100 DAYS AND 99 NIGHTS

100 DAYS AND 99 NIGHTS

A novel by Alan Madison

Illustrated by Julia Denos

LITTLE, BROWN AND COMPANY
Books for Young Readers
New York   Boston

Little, Brown and Company

Hachette Book Group USA
237 Park Avenue, New York, NY 10017
Visit our Web site at www.lb-kids.com

First Edition: May 2008

The characters and events portrayed in this book are fictitious. Any similarity
to real persons, living or dead, is coincidental and not intended by the author.

Library of Congress Cataloging-in-Publication Data

Madison, Alan.
100 days and 99 nights / by Alan Madison. — 1st ed.
p. cm.
Summary: As Esme introduces her stuffed animal collection that is
alphabetically arranged from Alvin the aardvark to Zelda the zebra she
also relates her family's military life and her father's deployment.
ISBN 978-0-316-11354-0
[1. Children of military personnel — Fiction. 2. Toys — Fiction.
3. Family life — Virginia — Fiction. 4. Imagination — Fiction. 5. Alexandria
(Va.) — Fiction.] I. Title. II. Title: One hundred days and ninety-nine nights.
PZ7.M2587On 2008
[Fic] — dc22
2007031543

10 9 8 7 6 5 4 3 2 1

RRD-C

Printed in the U.S.A.

Book design by Maria Mercado

★ ✦ ★

Dedicated to those who in every generation
have courageously remained to keep the
home fires burning.

And to four strong, Julie M., Karen K.,
Gail H., and Nancy C., whose support
keeps the fustilugs away.

It's Me, Esme!

Everyone calls me Esme, which is five letters short of my given name, Esmerelda. My middle name, Swishback, is my mother's last name before she got married. And my last name, McCarther, is spelled with two C's — the first one is a baby and the second one isn't. That's me all over: I'm Esmerelda Swishback McCarther.

I have one biggish brown dog named Napoleon; two smallish hairy hamsters, Grant who is white and Lee who is black; a bowl of goldfish; and one little brother we call "Ike" which is almost nearly two letters short of his given name, Isaac.

I love most every animal from whales to worms, with three exceptions: skunks, skinks, and my little brother, Ike. Skunks smell bad and skinks are lizardly and stick tight when they bite. Ike is a little like both.

On my bed, piled in a big mound over and around my pillow and down, is my A to Z, absolutely almost complete collection of stuffed animals. I have every letter, from A (aardvark) to Z (zebra) — except for X because there is no animal I have found that begins with that troublesome letter. The only words I know that even start that way are xylophone, x-ray, and x-actly.

I keep all my fuzzy animal friends in strict alphabet order starting from A (aardvark) on the left side of my pillow to Z (zebra) on the right and all the middling letters, L (lamb, lion), M (muskrat), and N (nightingale). Then O, P, Q, R, and S, running from the middle right down to the foot of my bed. Dad says that this is a very Swishback thing to do.

Sometimes, Ike comes into my room and for no good reason mixes them all up. Mom says this is a very Mc-Carther thing to do. I wish I could have Ike stuffed and keep him lying silent between my hippopotamus and my jaguar. But I don't think that would make my parents too happy.

The best part of my "bedzoo" (which is what my dad named my collection) is that each animal reminds me of someone or something special. For example, Alvin, my stuffed brown and slightly frayed aardvark, reminds me of Grandpa McCarther, gin rummy, and my missing appendix.

But my most loved possession of all, which I keep carefully hidden in the pouch of Katie my kangaroo, is the remains of what once was my pinkish-blue blanket.

When I was born, Grandma Swishback sent it to me special delivery. It used to be a full blanket with wonderfully woven stripes running across it, but now after my seven-plus years and four-plus countries in exactly four different continents, it is nothing more than a frayed scrap of pink threads tangled up in blue ones. I call it blankie and at night I hold it against my cheek to help me fall asleep.

Sometimes grown-ups can say the silliest things like, "Esme, aren't you too old to have a blankie?"

This makes me mad-sad, which is my worst feeling because it is one you can't do anything about. It is like being on a carousel that keeps going around and around getting faster and faster, and if you don't get off quick it makes you real nauseous. When I am mad that is okay because I can yell. Like the day when Ike came into my room (which, by the way, he is *not* allowed to do without my permission) and jumbled my animals.

"Isaac Swishback McCarther, I will mash you if you do that again!" I screeched, which sent him scurrying away and made me feel a little better.

When I am just sad, like when Ike said, "You are the worst sister in the whole wide world!" I can curl up with my animals, pull my pinkish-blue blankie scrap from Katie my kangaroo's pouch, and rub it against my cheek. This always makes me feel a little better. *Sometimes* when I am really sad I even cry. But just sometimes . . .

*   *   *

But with mad-sad there is nothing at all to do. Like the time our next-door neighbor, Mrs. Hadley, dropped off milk and eggs from the market once as a favor and asked, "Esme, aren't you too old to have a blankie?"

First I got mad and pounded my size fours up to my room and then I got sad and cried. Around and around, faster and faster, I went on this mad-sad carousel. Mom knocked and entered.

"Sometimes grown-ups can say the silliest things," she said. She scooped up my yak, unicorn, and zebra, moved them to her lap, sat in their spot, and stroked my hair from the top of my head down to its shoulder-length ends.

"People who don't think before they talk are called fustilugs. And we really must feel sorry for them."

For five seconds I stopped sobbing and raced through all the words I keep in my head to see if I had ever heard this one before. I most definitely had not. A new word is like a sweet butterscotch sucking candy — you have to enjoy every second of it because you will most probably only get one that day.

"Fustilugs — it rhymes with crusty bugs."

A short burst of hot wet air snorted from my nose, which is what happens when you laugh and cry at the same exact time.

"You see, darling, in the remote country of

Nostomania, in its very center, in its densest jungle, live long bandy-legged blue bugs, called fustilugs."

My mad-sad slowly crawled into plain curiosity. To hear better, I slid Hanna my hippo (missing her right button eye) over and propped my head up on her big butt.

"These crusty bugs enter in through the ears of sleeping adults who, even when they are awake, don't think very much, and then creep down deep into their heads."

My lips slight-separated in horror. Mom's hand ran reassuringly down my hair.

"They know it is safe, empty, and quiet in the head of an adult who doesn't think so much. Once inside, they spin their thick spiderish webs to make their nests. These silvery threads clog up the grown-up's brain and make it absolutely impossible for these thoughtless people to think of a sentence or even a word without actually saying it. These fustilugs, whose heads are now filled with the gummy webs of crusty blue bugs, live miserably, wandering from town to town without friends, 'cause whatever they think — they say. It is all so very sad."

My mom's a good storyteller.

Since Mom told me this sad bug tale, I have learned that it is best *not* to respond to a fustilug because they are just plain jealous, and probably deep down wish they had a blankie as special as mine. What Mom and I know that these fustilugs don't is that Grandma Swishback, who knit this for me, left us forever three years ago. So this scrap of blue and pink is the only thing I have that reminds me of her . . . I think it reminds Mom too.

* ◦ *

Dad says that along our path from home to home I've lost scraps of my blankie, so that if I ever wanted to find my way back to any one particular place I could retrace my steps by following the pinkish-blue shreds — just like in Hansel and Gretel. I didn't think it was much of a joke and frowned, turning the corners of my mouth super way down. Dad said I looked just like a Swishback when I frowned this way, which to him, a McCarther, was no great compliment.

My father, August Aloysius McCarther the Third, is a sergeant in the United States Army. His father, and my grandfather, August Aloysius McCarther the Second, was in the army, and his father's father, my great-grandfather, August Aloysius McCarther the very first, was also in the army. Dad says that McCarthers have been in the army since the beginning of time or at least since the beginning of "the good ol' U.S. of A."

That's what Dad likes to call it, "the good ol' U.S. of A."
When I'm old enough, I'll probably be in the army too.

In the army, you get to travel around a whole lot. Sometimes you're sent to really interesting places and sometimes . . . you're not.

Dad says that because of the army he stood shoulder to shoulder with polar bears and watched the sun rise over the frozen fields of Alaska, which sounds really exciting. And because of the army he slept in sludge, shoulder to shoulder with snakes, and watched the sun set over the swamps of Alabama — which does not.

Dad says that each state has its particular pleasures but if given the choice he prefers Alaska, standing with the bears. But the army doesn't really give you a choice and no matter where you're sent, you go, because when you're in the army you follow orders and you don't ever complain.

"Why?"

"In the army we don't ask why. We just do."

"Why?" I dared to ask again.

"That's just the way it is."

Which to me is an answer that leaves room for more questions at the same time that it leaves no room for more questions.

Aardvark

Grandpa McCarther brought me my soft stuffed aardvark, Alvin, when I was in the hospital when my appendix was angry. The doctors removed it (the appendix, not the aardvark) and as a reminder left me a scary little pink scar at the edge of my belly. Grandpa McCarther sat there the whole day reading me books and teaching me how to play gin rummy. He is a top-dog teacher but not such a good player. He lost most every game!

* ✿ *

When I was two, my family lived in Seoul, South Korea. Being a baby at the time, I don't remember boo about Korea except that it was ice-cream cold and most everywhere we went, we went bundled under a quilt, a coat, *and* a sweater! All the people who lived there were the crispy color of perfectly toasted marshmallows, like the ones that my dad made on the stove during those wintry Korean nights. All the people there didn't speak the language I spoke, so they didn't talk to me so often, but when they did, it wasn't so much like talking as it was like singing.

Since I was just a baby, I don't really actually know if I especially liked living in Korea, but when Mom and I flip through the photo albums she has carefully organized by month and year, from the time she was a little girl looking just like me, through when she knew Daddy but did not know me, to when I arrived, past all our trips, up to just about yesterday, I point out that I am smiling, so I must have liked it.

"You were a very happy baby," she remarks, raising her eyebrows in high arcs.

Mom didn't particularly like what she calls "our little Korean adventure."

When I turned three, we moved to Nairobi, Kenya. That's where Ike was born. I don't remember boo about Kenya, either, except that it was oatmeal hot and most everywhere we went, we never ever wore a quilt, a coat, a sweater, or even a shirt! Most everyone who lived there was the color of double deep chocolate frosting, the kind my mom spreads thick across the cake she makes on my birthday. With my paler freckled skin and straight lighter brown hair, I felt like I had landed from a faraway planet. Most everyone who lived there didn't speak the language I spoke, so they didn't talk to me so often, but when they did, it wasn't so much like talking as it was a hushed whisper.

I remember the sound of gallons of rain pounding on our roof during the noisy nights and the steady hiss of white steam rising off the ground during the super silent hot days. But mostly I remember our drives through the country, seeing real live rhinos, antelope, crocodiles, wildebeests, and even lions.

I don't really actually remember if I liked living in Kenya, but I am smiling in the photos, so I must have.

"You were a very happy toddler," Mom says again, making her eyebrows into high arcs.

I don't think she really, truly liked what she calls "our little Kenyan adventure" either.

Whenever we have to move to new country my dad calls Mom, me, and Ike into the kitchen, which is the most important room in our house because that's where we do all our most excellent cooking and all our most serious talking, and says, "Okay, troops, it's time to pack up and head out."

Then Mom reminds us in her funny but strict voice, which is the tone she takes when she means something serious but wants to pretend it is a joke, "No questions asked."

"Because no answers will be given!" adds Dad in his big booming sergeant voice, as if we were his actual soldiers. This is the voice he uses to make us feel very important — and it does.

So we pack up and head out without a peep.

When I was five we moved to Frankfurt, Germany, and when I was six we were sent to Hamburg, also in Germany. I felt that these were very tasty places to live because I liked eating frankfurts and hamburgs.

Germany was oatmeal hot in the summer and ice-cream cold in the winter. Sometimes we needed a quilt, a coat, and a sweater, and sometimes we didn't. Most everyone who lived there was the color of the pale milk Mom pours over my breakfast cereal.

Most everyone there didn't speak the language I spoke, so they didn't speak to me so often, but when they did, it wasn't so much like talking as it was like they were guard-dog-barking.

"Esmerelda Swishback McCarther! That is not very nice at all."

Well, that is what it sounded like to me!

I would practice their words by making the far back of my throat vibrate until sounds like *aaacchhhhh* and *ooocchhhh* would rumble out.

*　　*　　*

I really actually remember living in Frankfurter and Hamburger and don't have to check my frown in the photo albums to know that I really didn't like "our little German adventure" too much.

I was never really positive what people were saying to me and I'm pretty sure they weren't so positive about what I was saying to them. So even though I had Ike, Napoleon, Grant and Lee, Mom, Dad, my A to Z bedzoo, and my scraggly blankie, I was a little — just a little — lonely.

When I turned lucky seven my dad called us into the kitchen, which I think I have mentioned is the most important room in our house because that's where we do all our super important cooking and all our serious talking, and said, "Okay, troops, it's time to pack up and head out. We are going back to the good ol' U.S. of A."

So we did.

Bandicoot

All that we owned we packed into big brown boxes — even my stuffed bandicoot, Berta (who I named after my friend in Hamburg who gave her to me). Bandicoots are from a down-under island called Australia. The encyclopedia says they are a cross between a pig and a rat, which does not seem like such a good combination, but my bandicoot has a long hairy nose and big flop-elephant ears and is very cute.

✦ ❂ ✦

The movers loaded all our boxes into a long truck that drove to the hugest airplane that brought the boxes across the very biggest blue ocean.

From our new German cuckoo clock to our old Korean kimonos, all was sent to America that way except our dog, Napoleon (my father carried him over his shoulder); our hamsters, Grant and Lee (Ike careful-carried one in each coat pocket); and my extra special Grandma Swishback blankie (I carried it in my fist). I would never, could never, will never, no matter how many times we travel, pack my blankie in any size brown box, thank you very much.

Sadly, my three favorite goldfish didn't make it through all our travels. In Seoul, South Korea, Hannibal jumped the bowl. He was stone-still stiff when Mom found him by barefoot-stepping on him the next morning. That was some scream. After saying some sad words and complimenting him on what a good pet he had been, we buried him out back in the ice-crispy dirt.

"*Ahn nyung hee ke se yo*, honorable Hannibal," said Dad. In Korean, that means "Goodbye, Hannibal." Then he saluted sharply, which in the military means "We'll miss you."

In Kenya, Alexander belly-floated to the top of the tank. Dad discovered him first and ladled him out. Bowing our heads, we cried and teary-told about what a fine pet he had been, then buried him out back in the sun-warmed sand.

"*Kwa heri*, Alexander," Mom sad-stated, which means "Goodbye, Alexander" in Swahili, the language of Kenya. Then she saluted, which means "We'll miss you" in the language of the military.

In Frankfurt, no one discovered Julius. He just vanished. We searched the floor around the bowl, under the rocks in the bowl, and inside the little green-and-red sand-castle that squatted in the center of the bowl. No orange Julius. He had disappeared.

Ike figured that Julius was lonely and had packed his few possessions in a little fish suitcase and taken a tiny fish train back to the pond to visit his friends. I call this type of thinking "Ike Sense," which is the kind that makes no sense at all.

"Ike probably ate him," Dad teased, and I believed him. Ike would eat just about anything. Mom didn't think it was much of a joke and frowned at the two of us.

"Uh-oh, I'm in trouble," Dad moaned, reacting to her stony Swishback stare.

"We are just unlucky when it comes to fish. End of story," she declared.

And it was.

"*Ah veterzane*, Julius," I proclaimed, which meant "Goodbye, Julius" in German. Ike saluted the now empty bowl, which meant we needed new fish for our new start in the good ol' U.S. of A.

Cat, Cow, Camel

There are twenty-six letters in the A to Z alphabet (only twenty-five with the missing X), but I have many more than twenty-five stuffed animals. For some letters, like C, I have three animals: a calico cat that my mother brought me when I was home with a cough, a brown-spotted cow that we got when we drove through Kansas, and a camel my never-met cousin Catherine sent me for my sixth birthday.

* ◎ *

If I stand on my tiptoes on the tiptop stone steps of my new school in Alexandria, Virginia, I can see the pretty point at the top of the Washington Monument, and if I stand on my tiptoes on the top wooden steps of my back porch, I can see the capped columns of the White House, where the President lives.

Most everyone who lives here speaks the language I speak, but they sound completely different. When they talk they take entirely too much time saying vowels, like when they call me "Y'aaall" or ask if they can pet my "daawg." Grandpa McCarther says I'll get used to people's "draawl" and before you know it will be talking with extra-long vowels too.

I say, "Nooo waaay!" slow-stringing out all the O's and A's in such a Southern drawl that it makes Grandpa laugh.

Our new house is very different from all the other houses we have lived in around the world because it feels like home. For the first time, I have my own room, Ike has his own room, and Mom and Dad have their own room too! There is an upstairs, a downstairs, and even stairs to a deep-down-in-the-ground basement that's a perfect place for me to keep my wood building blocks and Ike to keep his collection of trucks.

The fenced-in backyard is a little square of patio mixed with grass that is too small for hide-and-seek but just wide enough for freeze tag. Dad built a little wooden doghouse in the far corner and Ike painted in black box letters N P L N over the rounded entrance. "Dogs can't read vowels," he explains, which is his first amazing display of Ike Sense in the good ol' U.S. of A.

"Dogs can't read at all," I growl. "I think it's mostly because you . . ."

But before I can finish saying that he doesn't know which vowels to put or where to put them, Mom throws me a freeze-you-in-your-tracks, immediate-interrupting, Swishback frown that leaves me mumbling to myself while Ike, whistling happily, crawls into our doghouse to play with Napoleon.

* ◌ *

Every morning in our new house, everything happens just about the same as the morning before it. Mom calls this our "morning routine." I like the word *routine* because it rolls out of my mouth like a rhyme. I also like what it means: doing things unchanged every time. And I very much like having it because then there is a plan every school morning. As Dad says, "Having a plan is fun-da-men-tal," which is a longish grown-up word for "very important."

I always wake up and get into the bathroom first. After I finish washing but before I brush my teeth, Ike pounds on the door with his fist.

"Esme, hurry or I'm going to be late for school!"

"You should have gotten up earlier," I slow-remind him, and continue to carefully brush my tops and bottoms from back to front. Ike, steam coming out of his ears 'cause he can't get in, runs to tattle to Dad that I am hogging the bathroom. Before he can get back to tell me, "Esme, you better hurry cause Dad is coming to kick you out," I am already gone. This always

makes even more steam come out of Ike's now burning red ears.

My clothes laid out the night before, I quickly get dressed, make sure my homework is in my backpack, place my scrap of blankie carefully in Katie's pouch, arrange all of my A to Z stuffed animals properly in their bedzoo, and trot down the stairs to eat my cold cereal breakfast. When the big hand swipes the twelve with the little hand pointing to eight, the newspaper hits our front door. *Thud!* The sound is like a light switch that turns on our parents. They immediately come rumbling down the stairs in a big rush, jumbling their words and juggling their bags.

My father gives us top-of-the-head kisses, orders us off to school with a "have a great day," and like many of the other fathers on our block drives away to work.

Every morning my mother does the exact opposite: she drives us to school like many of the other mothers on the block, and then gives us "have a great day" hugs and right-cheek kisses. Either way is okay by me because sooner or later we get our kisses.

Dad says that at work he marches his soldiers around and around all day, every day. He jokes that when they get tired he makes them march asquare. When Ike and

I don't laugh, he explains that you can march soldiers "around" but you can't march them "asquare," because really there is no such thing.

"It's a joke," he explains, and we nod and smile. We don't want to hurt his feelings. Dads like to tell those types of not-so-funny jokes.

Every day at school, my teacher, Ms. Pitcher, makes us read and write, and when we get tired we do arithmetic. She *never* marches us.

Every day at home, my mother cleans up the house, shops for food, and then writes a story. She says she marches all right, but to her "very own beat." I'm not sure what that means but it makes me smile inside when I imagine the way it would look.

My mother, Penelope Lulu Swishback McCarther, is a reporter for the *Drum & Bugle*, the monthly newspaper for all the soldiers and their families. Her mother, Bernice Lorelei Swishback, my grandmother, was a reporter for the *Weekly Gazette*, which was the weekly newspaper for all the families of Midway, Missouri. Her mother's mother, my great-grandmother, whom I was named after, Esmerelda Louisa Hockenfuss, was also a reporter, but for the *Daily Telegraph*, which came out each morning for all the families of Argonne, Oregon.

Mommy says that her family has been working in news-papers since the beginning of time or at least since the beginning of newspapers.

When I'm old enough, and no longer in the army, I'll probably work in newspapers too.

Diana Moon Duck

My babysitter in South Korea, Hong Moonduk, which was as funny a name to me as Esmerelda Swishback McCarther was to her, gave me a stuffed duck before we left for Dad's next post. I named her Diana Moon Duck and placed her in the center of my pillow. Hong felt this was quite an honor and bowed her head slightly to tell me so.

* ☼ *

Saturday is my favorite day of the week because there is no school and there is absolutely no army. It's also the morning my dad cooks us breakfast. Pancakes.

From Tallahassee to Tokyo, every corporal and colonel knows that my dad makes the absolute tastiest top-dog pancakes from a top secret recipe that was handed down from his father, August Aloysius McCarther the Second, my grandfather, who got it from his father's father, my great-grandfather, August Aloysius Mc-Carther the very first.

*   *   *

When I'm old enough, I'll probably make extra tasty, top-dog pancakes too. But until then, I just help my dad.

I am best at beating the batter, Ike is best at greasing the griddle, and Dad is, of course, far and away the finest flipper between here and just about anywhere. While we are working, Mom sits sipping coffee and reading the *Drum & Bugle*. She makes sure that there are no mistakes in either the newspaper or the manner in which we prepare pancakes. Dad says she is a "super supervisor."

To make sure our pancakes come out consistently top-dog tasty, it is extremely important to do everything precisely the same way it was done the Saturday before, and the Saturday before that, and before that. To do this we follow Dad's pancake rules.

See, my dad has rules for just about everything: there's the playground rules, the travel rules, the many, many school rules, and the very crucial cooking pancake rules. Like routines, "Rules are fun-da-men-tal," he says, "because when things start to go wrong you can always count on rules to save you. This way there are things you don't even have to think about — you just follow the rules."

He calls these things "no-brainers."

"No-brainers! How's about no-stomachers! Or no-nosers!" Ike snorts and laughs, then proceeds through the whole body from eyes to toes before Dad stops him.

"If you have hard-and-fast rules that you always follow, it leaves more room in your head to think about important things," he explains precisely to the still-giggling Ike.

Dad learned all this rule business in the army, where there are more rules "than you can shake a stick at." I'm not sure what the "shake a stick at" part means, but Dad says it a lot.

Our routine on the weekend is really different from our school days. There are no alarms set, so we wake up late, there's no yelling about the bathroom, no newspaper *thud*, no rushing, jumbling, or juggling, and best of all, there is no cold cereal.

Saturday mornings, when the cuckoo clock begins the first of eight cuckoos, Ike and I slip downstairs, drop our aprons over our heads, and tie the string over our bellies, each with the exact same double-looped bow. We try to finish before the mechanical bird sticks its tiny red-tufted head out to deliver the final high-pitched cuckoo.

While we wash our hands in the kitchen sink, Dad, in his green-and-yellow-squared flannel robe, rubbing the top of his buzz-cut head, pounds down the stairs. Blinking the sleep from his eyes, he inspects our cooking uniforms. When satisfied, he yawns, "Okay, troops, we are ready to cook."

We salute, bringing our open right hands sharply to our foreheads and then karate chopping them down. This is military speak for "ready, willing, and able." Dad says we should always end it with "sir, yes, sir," to show the proper respect for a commanding officer.

"Sir, yes, sir!" Ike and I cry in unison.

"One cup flour," he commands.

"Flour is made from flowers," Ike states as usual.

Dad smiles and I roll my eyes around my head because *every* week Ike always swears that flour (F-L-O-U-R) is made from flowers (F-L-O-W-E-R-S) and that is why they are spelled differently. This makes zero sense, which is exactly Ike Sense, because then they should be spelled exactly the same!

"Actually, Ike, flour and flower are spelled differently because they are quite different things," explains Dad patiently for the umpteenth time. "Flour — F-L-O-U-R — comes from wheat, which is a plant but really doesn't have flowers — F-L-O-W-E-R-S — at all."

"No, Dad, I am absolutely, positively sure of it, they are the same." Ike continues to insist, then dumps the cup of *flour* into the bowl.

Under Dad's watchful eye, we exact-measure and combine the salt and baking soda into the bowl. Then, trying not to make too much of a mess, we carefully measure out the wet ingredients: water, oil, and the top secretest ingredient — "Yogurt!" Ike yells. "Yogurt, yoooguurt!" he screams. Ike feels that *yogurt* is the absolute funniest word he has ever heard and as soon as dad starts spooning out the glistening white goo, he starts giggling and rolling the word out of his mouth, either drawing out the soft-sounding "yo" or cutting off the hard-syllabled "gurt" and sometimes even attempting to do both. "Yoooogrt!" Mom chuckles from behind the spread-open *Drum & Bugle* as Ike goes through his word acrobatics while I remain silent because I feel *llama* is an even funnier word.

Dad knows a lot of funny words, but during pancake making he is always partial to *spatula.*

"Spaaatulllaaa, spa-chew — la, sssspit-u-laaa." He bounces the word over and over, making it funnier and funnier until Ike and I are both laughing so hard we nearly fall off our stools.

"Augie, the pancakes, please," Mom warns.

Dad stops and, wearing Napoleon's bad-dog look, drags back to the batter.

* * *

I wooden-spoon-mix together all the ingredients, from the Ike Sense–spelled flour to the somewhat funny-named yogurt, while Ike quick-drops pats of butter onto the hot griddle. Mom super-supervises this part, letting out an *aaahh* sound of approval each time Ike places a pat correctly and an *ooo-ooo-ooo* sound of disapproval each time his hand comes down too close to the stove.

Dad big-spoons batter onto the burning black metal. It flattens and soon little bubbles begin bursting. After we count out five of these tiny explosions, Dad does the famous fancy McCarther flip. He skillfully slides his "spaaatuulaaa" under one round and snaps his wrist, revealing both the colorful tattoo on his wide forearm and the brown cooked side of the perfect pancake.

A most definite Dad cooking rule is: "Neither a borrower nor a lender be." This means that when it comes to a particular pancaking post, whether it is buttering, mixing, or flipping, you have your very own job to do, and you should never ever trade or even ask to trade — you just do your job. Our cooking tasks have become total no-brainers and given the excellent eating results, I have to say that Dad's pancaking rules most definitely do work.

The short stacks are piled high on each of our plates, the maple syrup slow-flowed, and the only sounds heard are the rushed clicks and clacks of forks on plates and the rumble of satisfied *ummms.*

Then, after the full rounds are reduced to last bites, we start to talk over the past week's victories and defeats, chores for the day, and challenges for next week.

"How was school this week?"

"I had a spelling quiz."

"Me too."

I twist my lips at Ike's false chorus.

"On Wednesday I will pick you both up right after school. You both have dentist appointments," Mom said.

Ugh! I think.

"Uchhh," Ike phlegms, nearly choking on his last bite.

"Young man," warns Dad, and slides seconds onto our plates. Without further fuss we return to eating and dig into our second stack.

This is an absolute authentic account of how every Saturday we, the Swishback McCarthers, would cook the tastiest pancakes in the whole world.

Well, until *that* Saturday.

Elephant

My father's older brother, Uncle Colin, who Mom does not really like because he sometimes tells bad fibs, and my aunt Alma, who Mom really likes because she doesn't, gave me Edgar my elephant for my fifth birthday. Edgar reminds me that fibbing can get you into big trouble. Fibbing, which is a lot like lying, is the worst thing you can do in our house. It will automatically earn you a trip to your room and a long lecture.

* ✿ *

It was a Saturday morning in the kitchen like all others before it. We were beating the batter and beginning the butter when my father, the finest flipper from Fiji to France, put his spatula down and his thick arms around us.

"Esmerelda, Isaac . . ."

Oh, no, I inside-fretted. Anytime he called us by our full first names, something big happened, like we'd get another pet or . . . move to another country. Napoleon left his spot next to the fireplace and slow-walked closer, head down, probably expecting to hear that we were adopting the stray cat that wandered our block, or . . .

"I have to go away," he said immediately, so as not to make us worry any longer.

"We're moving again!" moaned Ike.

"No . . . no, this time I have to go alone."

It was scary silent except for the angry hiss of butter skiing across the skillet.

"We're not moving?" I asked, relieved and worried at the same exact moment.

"No. I have to go to a faraway place for one hundred days and ninety-nine nights," he answered in his most deeply serious voice.

All I could think to say was, "That's a long time." So I said it: "That's a long time."

For a second I feared that last night bandy-legged blue bugs from the remotest jungles of Nostomania had crept into my head and I had become a fustilug destined to say whatever came to mind without any thought of how it might hurt someone else's feelings. But Dad calmed my fears.

He slid his hand onto my shoulder and answered directly, "Yes, it is. I don't want to leave you but it is my duty."

"Duty" is what the army calls it when you have to do something that no one in the whole entire universe really wants to do.

"But why?" asked Ike, who was too young to under-stand the word *duty* and old enough to really love the word *why.*

Our minds raced around the short silence, trying to figure out possible reasons for his leaving.

"Because my commander says so, and when he says so, in the army we just do."

He spooned the batter onto the sizzling skillet. The small circles sputtered and spit. When he stepped to the side he revealed my mom sitting at the kitchen table, the *Drum & Bugle* unopened, weak smile, eyes rimmed red. She must have been crying and looked like she was going to start to cry again, but she didn't. It was her duty not to cry in front of us. So I did my duty and I didn't cry in front of Ike, and since I didn't — Ike didn't. So we sat, doing our duty, holding our tears tight inside, heads down, concentrating on swishing the re-mains of our pancakes in the brown swamp of thick syrup on our plates. We didn't talk about what had hap-pened that week, or what was happening that day, or most especially what was going to happen. This Satur-day morning was silent except for the sizzle of the last batch of McCarther pancakes.

Frog

One vacation, we drove all the way from Frankfurt to France. Since Ike and I never even asked once, "Are we there yet?" we were allowed to pick out souvenirs. Ike grabbed a snow-filled globe with a tall pointy tower at its center and I chose my frog and named him Freddie. In France they sometimes get so hungry they eat frogs' legs, so by bringing Freddie back to Germany, where they do not eat such things, I had saved his life.

* ☉ *

That night, climbing into bed, my room seemed to get darker faster, as if it were winter times two. I organized my bedzoo, putting my three lucky C's (Cassie my camel, Cary my cat, and Cory my cow) across the top of my headboard to watch over me. Staring at the blank ceiling, I squeezed my limp blankie hard and pulled Freddie my frog close to my belly.

Dad soft-knocked and eased past the door. Nearing the bed, he leaned down and scooped up my long-haired lion, Larry, and my long-tailed squirrel, Sylvester, and wedged them back among my other animals that stared up at me from the foot of my bed. He tucked the covers tightly to my chin, then sat on the edge. The mattress slanted hard under his weight and several animals slid back to the floor.

"Esme, you're going to have to help your mother around here," he ordered and asked in the same exact sentence.

I understood and nodded in the same exact motion.

"Especially on Saturday mornings, because, as we know, your mother is a Swishback and Swishbacks don't make perfect pancakes." He grinned, herded a stray strand of hair back behind my ear, and left his warm hand to cup the side of my face.

"On Saturday mornings, you'll be the boss. You'll have to remind them that there are rules for pancakes." He brought the left corner of his mouth slightly up toward his ear to form a lopsided grin.

"That's a big responsibility for someone your age."

"Yes, sir," I replied in my most military voice, to try and assure him that I was absolutely one hundred percent "can-do."

"Every day you look more and more like your mother," Dad commented, which made me feel good because she is a very pretty mother. He gave me a peck on my forehead to try and assure me that he knew I was absolutely one hundred percent "can-do."

The fullish moon outside my window barely lit the tattoo on his right forearm. I closed my eyes tight so I could memorize every detail of it. A robin, its red chest proudly puffed, perched on the edge of a twig nest with a long wiggling worm squeezed in her beak. At her feet sat two small baby birds, mouths open wide, anxiously awaiting their meal. No one really knew for sure exactly what it meant. Grandpa McCarther had the same tattoo though. He said that McCarthers have gotten that particular mark since the beginning of time or at least since they began joining the army — which to him was probably the same thing. I half worried that one day I would have to get that tattoo and half wanted to one day get it too.

Dad smoothed my tangle of brown hair, his soft strokes pushing me toward sleep. I remembered a beach in Kenya where the sand was so boiling hot we could not get back to our blanket without burning the bottoms of our feet. I could see it and feel it as if I were there and not tucked into my bed here. Mom tried but couldn't carry little Ike and me across the sand at the same time. Dad came running, almost flying, and scooped us up. I remember watching the baby robins on his forearm frantically jumping, trying to reach the worm but never quite reaching it. He carried us for what must have been a mile, maybe more, or maybe not so far at all, but he did deliver us safely to our blanket and then even raced back to get Mom!

To me that tattooed robin meant that my dad, August Aloysius McCarther the Third, was the strongest, bravest person alive.

When I opened my eyes, he had turned and started away.

"Daddy," I said, just a tad too loud, then said just a tad too low, "take this with you."

I held out the tangled web of pink and blue cotton that was my treasured blankie.

"I'd be honored. But won't you need it?"

"I think you will need it more."

"You're a very courageous girl, Esmerelda Swishback McCarther. One day you'll make a great soldier."

"You won't forget to bring it back?"

He shook his head, sharp-saluted, and marched away.

I think every single one of my animals wanted to cry, from my frayed aardvark, Alvin, to Zelda, my zebra. I pulled my goat, Gabriella, closer; her usually clear eyes began to fog, and my walrus, Wallace's, marble eyeballs got moist. I knew that if I started even a whimper they, all thirty-two of them, would join in. We would most surely wake the entire neighborhood with our sad cries and lonely howls and fill my bed with tears. Under the covers I squeezed Pete my python's tail tight, then dug my nails into my palm, so I wouldn't cry. And since I didn't, they didn't.

Goat

My dad's best buddy is Supply Sergeant Gabe Sutler. Dad says he has known him since "basic" (which is the beginning of being in the army). Gabe's job is to make sure every soldier has everything they need, from butter to bullets. By accident, a company once sent Gabe a box of stuffed goats instead of a crate of overcoats. This was unlucky for the army but lucky for me.

* ◎ *

"**O**ne hundred days and ninety-nine nights is a long time," Ms. Pitcher, my teacher, threw out to the class. "How many daddies or mommies are away?"

Open hands sprouted like spring flowers. Arthur's father was in the air force and Martina's mom was in the marines, Pedro's pop was in the paratroopers and Bridget's older brother was in the navy.

I wasn't alone.

"Why?" Ms. Pitcher pop-quizzed. "Why?"

That was a hard question. *Why*, I wondered. There

was a war. He was in the army. The president. Duty. He was a McCarther. To protect me . . .

"Because that's how long a tour of duty is," replied Pedro. "When they go to fight they are sent for one hundred days and ninety-nine nights. After they do this, they come home."

"Very good, Pedro. A tour of duty."

"It's a long time." The words rolled heavily from my lips and lazy-lolled across my desk.

"Not really, Esme, no. If you look at these days differently it will go by — like that." Ms. Pitcher snapped her fingers to emphasize the "like that" part.

"One hundred days and ninety-nine nights sounds like forever, but it is also only fifteen Saturdays, and that doesn't. And if you say three months, well, that doesn't seem like a long haul at all."

Arthur, Pedro, Martina and me all forced smiles and gratefully agreed, but no matter how our teacher added, subtracted, multiplied, or divided the days, to us, it was still an awfully long time.

After lunch, Martina and I playground-played on the seesaw. We tried to count one hundred times up and ninety-nine times down, but somewhere around fifty we would forget and have to start again.

Martina and I were best friends. We sat across from each other in class, sat across from each other at lunch, and sat across from each other on the seesaw during recess. She had long brown hair and short brown eyes, just like me. And light brown skin and heavy brown eyebrows, not at all like me.

Ms. Pitcher said we were like "two peas in a pod." We had no idea what she meant, and since neither of us really liked peas we didn't consider it any sort of compliment. But since Ms. Pitcher was a grown-up and our teacher and we mostly liked her, we forced smiles and sort of agreed.

"Let's play king and queen," Martina requested. One of the reasons we liked each other so much was because we both loved to play made-up games.

"And they are our villagers!" I added, motioning to our playground-scattered classmates.

Slowly and carefully, I eased off my side of the "see" and then pushed down with all my weight to gently let her off her side, the "saw."

We climbed the cold metal bars to the top of the jungle gym, where we could see our whole playground kingdom.

Pedro and Arthur were playing catch in the far corner. Bridget and her little brother, Walter, were wandering near the swings. Richie C. and Georgina B., whom Martina and I did not get along with so much, were hogging the water fountain. Ike was trampolining his butt against the chain-link fence, arguing with his friend Stony Jackson. For best friends they sure liked to argue a lot.

"Ike!" I yelled to get his attention, but the playground was too loud. Stony was tiny for his age, and Ike tall for his, so he towered over his friend. But Stony was "tough as nails and had a chip on his shoulder." At least that is what Dad had once admiringly observed while we were sitting on the front stoop watching them play-wrestle. Dads can be silly.

The two boys stopped arguing and scrambled happily around the swings, playing tag.

"You be the queen," Martina barely suggested and mostly ordered.

"On Monday you were the teacher and I was the student — remember?" I reminded her.

"But yesterday you were the princess and I was the evil stepped-on sister!"

"Evil stepsister." As soon as the correction slipped my lips, I realized I shouldn't have said that and that I would be the queen today.

"Okay, I'll be the queen first. Then how about we switch in the middle?" After being mean and correcting her, the best I could hope for was halvsies.

"Cool."

We stood atop the bars of the jungle gym barking orders to our loyal subjects, who scurried this way and that.

"I want to have a royal ball that will be remembered forever!" Martina grandly announced.

"A dress of gold and diamonds for your queen!

"Bring me my magic sword!

"Bring me my ruby crown!"

Food, sodas, shoes, jewels, clowns, and music. We commanded and planned, ordered and laughed, imagining every last detail of the grand ball. Then as our dessert of chocolate strawberries, chocolate cake, and chocolate ice cream was being served, the end-of-recess bell rang. Balancing on the round bar, Martina rose up to give a final order. She swept her hand across her body and commanded, "To war! Follow my magic sword and defend our castle."

"All to battle. Defend your queen and king!" I added so enthusiastically that I lost my balance and wobbled down onto the bars, barely catching myself from falling farther.

Across our playground kingdom, our pretend villagers and very real classmates scooped up their book bags and streamed toward the big metal push doors where our arm-crossed teachers waited.

"To war! To war!" we again urged.

Martina and I laughed and laughed at the shoving students trying to funnel into the doorway. Exhausted, gasping for breath, we sat hooking our feet under a bar and watched the final boys, who had been playing basketball at the far end fence. Giggling, playfully pushing,

still rhythmic ball-bouncing, they disappeared through the doors.

"To war . . . ," Martina barely whispered under her breath, breaking the momentary quiet of the emptied playground.

"To war . . . ," I soft-echoed to no one in particular.

"You girls get down right this minute. Martina! Esme! Recess is over."

This direct order set Martina's mouth straight. Sad at being relieved of command, she dropped to the ground.

On top of the jungle gym in the middle of the empty school playground, for one single moment, I was really alone. Half that moment felt really good, and then for the other half it felt really, really scary.

"Esmerelda! Now!"

Hippo, Horsey

Hanna my hippo (missing her right button eye) and Harry my horsey (rip on his left rear hoof) are the oldest animals in my bedzoo. They were given to me when I was first born, and Mom says that they have "seniority," which is a long word that means that they should be respected since they have been around the longest. And they are! Parents sometimes make up long, serious words for such short, simple things.

* ✺ *

The first days that Dad was gone flew fast, like I was on a galloping horse. Those were the easy days. When I missed him first thing in the morning I pretended that he had gone to an early meeting. When he didn't come home at night I pretended he was away for just a few days on "maneuvers." This was when he and his unit painted their faces green and went to a nearby forest and pretended there was a fight in that forest so that if there ever were a fight in a forest like that one they would pretty much be ready. It was something he did every few months and it sounded pretty fun.

I imagined him upstairs in the attic when I was downstairs in the basement. In the kitchen cooking dinner when I was in the bathroom taking my bath. When I was outside in the backyard playing freeze tag with my friends he was inside watching the football game with Grandpa. In my mind we just kept missing bumping into each other by a minute or two. "Bad luck," I would mumble to myself, and go on my way.

Although the first days were easier for me, they were harder for Ike. Even though he can be both a skunk and a skink, I felt bad and tried as hard as I could to help.

"Pretend he went to the supermarket and he'll be right back," I explained one morning when Ike was particularly blue.

Ike did and smiled — for five minutes before the dark thundercloud of real memory crossed back over his face. Poor Ike, if only he could imagine like me.

But then, as the days began to fall like raindrops, I couldn't keep running between them and pretending I was not getting wet. So, as each day got easier for Ike because he had gotten used to being soaked, it got worse for me. Soon I was drenched and shivering.

*   *   *

One night when Ike and I were having dinner and Mom was in the shower, the phone rang.

"Hello, may I speak with your daddy?" asked a man's voice.

"One second," I replied out of habit.

"Thank you. I'll hold."

I put the phone down on the counter, turned to yell "Dad!" and swallowed the word whole as I realized what I had done, and now I didn't know what to do. Ike slow-turned to me from the table, his mouth filled with steak and potatoes. "'At'sa atter?"

I didn't know what to do. The phone lay there. Mom was upstairs. And Ike just stared.

"It's for Dad."

"He's not here."

"I know, but I . . . forgot."

Ike slurped up a final forkful of green beans and circled around me to the phone.

"Hello? He's . . ."

The man on the other end of the line interrupted Ike thinking he was Dad and started to talk and talk. I watched Ike listen and listen and every few seconds try to say something to set him straight. But I could hear the man just keep on talking.

"Ike? Who is it?" Mom stood at the door toweling her hair. Ike shrugged. Mom made her squishy concerned face and opened her hand for the phone. Ike passed it to her. I could still hear the man on the other end talking.

"Hello? Yes, who is this? No, I'm sorry, we are not . . . no . . . I'm sure the Caribbean is beautiful but . . . I'm sorry, we are not interested." And before the man could say another word, she hung up.

"Very funny, Ike." She crossed to the sink to start washing the dishes. "A Caribbean cruise. Very funny indeed. Finish your dinner, you two."

After answering that one call I couldn't pretend anymore that it was just "bad luck" that I kept missing Dad and I started to just miss Dad. And after Mom hung up the phone I made my very first rule: Don't answer the phone. So I didn't.

With Dad gone, every day passed at a hippo's clumping pace. After dinner I crisscrossed off each date from the calendar thumbtacked above my bed. Then I dove down between my covers and tried to sleep. There was no blankie to cuddle, so instead each night I adopted one of my stuffed animals. I started with A (aardvark) and was up to I (inchworm).

When I finished the alphabet with Zelda my zebra, I'd just start again.

*　　*　　*

Tight-gripping Ida my inchworm's ear, I wished my father, Sergeant August Aloysius McCarther the Third, had tucked me in. Then I squeeze-closed my eyes and dreamed my wish.

Inchworm

When I lost my absolute first tooth, the tooth fairy gave me Ida my inchworm. She is much longer than an inch and has green and yellow fuzz and a big red-mouthed smile. I put my tooth under the pillow and the next morning the tooth was gone and Ida had inched into its place. Back then, I believed in the tooth fairy.

* ◯ *

I shoveled clumpy mounds of brown-sugared oatmeal into my mouth and angrily stewed at Ike while he, on purpose to bother me, poked at his.

Every morning everything happened differently from the morning before it. With Dad away there was no "routine."

Sometimes Ike would wake before me, sometimes he wouldn't. Sometimes he'd pound on the bathroom door, sometimes he wouldn't. Sometimes cereal was out, sometimes it wasn't. I looked up at the clock when the big hand clicked upright to the twelve.

That was the same. *Thud!* That was the same. Yes. The newspaper hit the front door. But now the switch had broken. Ike lazily played with his food. The stairs silent, the muffled scuffling sound of Mom getting dressed upstairs, no big rush, no jumble of words, no juggling of bags. No "routine." No fun-da-men-tal plan.

"Eat," I instructed.

"You're not my boss," he snappped, and then stuck his oatmealed tongue out at me.

"Yes, I am," I stated, thinking I should have the same "seniority" here that Hippo and Horsey had in my bedzoo.

"No, you're not."

"Yes, I am."

"No, you're not."

If our father were here he'd administer Ike an A1 immediate attitude adjustment.

"Isaac Aloysius Swishback McCarther, you apologize to your sister this minute and eat your oatmeal, young man. Or you will find yourself . . ."

I listed the delicious menu of choice punishments: in the corner, in your room, no TV, to bed early . . . Ike would apologize fast. My skinky brother had stubbornly refused to do what I commanded and was still just pushing and pulling his now cold oats.

I looked over to Dad's chair. Since it was empty I could see past it to the corner of our kitchen counter where a stack of unopened mail addressed to him was piled high.

"Eat."

"Why?"

"It is your duty," I exactly explained because I know he sometimes forgets.

"Doodeee!!" He howled. "Doodeee!" he repeated, and ran upstairs, laughing, basketball-bouncing the word over and over and over in his mouth as if it were funnier than *yogurt, llama,* and *spatula* all smushed together.

"Yogullamatula," I weakly yelled after him.

"Doodee! Doodee!" he yelled down the stairwell in his annoying super-squeaky voice.

"Ike Sense," I tried to reassure myself, but couldn't. Not liking his behavior one bit, I stomped upstairs to report the event to my mother. I pushed open her door. At the foot of her bed she was doing the jumpy dance she does while pulling on her panty hose.

"Isaac Swishback McCarther did not finish his breakfast *AND* he stuck out his tongue at me with food on it! Uchhh." As soon as I said it I wanted to slurp the words back but I couldn't, so instead I kept going. "And then, and then, and then, he kept making fun of the word *duty!* It is not a funny word. Not even nearly as funny as *llama.* Not even close. He just doesn't understand how important that word is!"

Then, like an unknotted birthday balloon that had just finished whizzing the room, I plopped onto the corner of my dad's side of the bed.

Flowery print skirt crumpled around her hips like a

life preserver, Mom finished yanking her stretchy panty hose into place, then rested her hands on my shoulders and rubbed them.

"You have to remember he is still too young to really understand the meaning of some very important words. Wouldn't you say?"

I nodded, too tired to answer with words.

"BUT, missy," she continued sternly, "don't be a tattletale."

Ouch, I thought to myself. A tattletale. That's what I sounded like? A tattletale. One single step above a fustilug. Wasn't I in charge when my parents weren't around? Why was it tattling when it was clearly Ike who was way wrong? Not fair!

"Now, let's get going. Shoes on, backpack packed. We'll talk more about this later. We're going to be late for school."

I did an about-face and fast-turned into my room. Stray animals, dirty clothes, books, and dolls dotted the pink carpeting. At that moment the whole mess seemed like it was absolutely my elephant, Edgar's, fault. I kicked him and he tumbled trunk over tail into the darkness under my bed. *Anyway, he was not a real live animal,* I thought as I got dressed.

Not being a tattletale was definitely a Dad rule, but if Dad were here he would definitely make Ike understand about duty.

Jaguar

My first nursery school teacher gave Julian my jet-black jaguar to me in Kenya. She said jaguars moved the most beautifully of all the animals.

* ❂ *

Unlike home, school was still mostly the same routine. My teacher, Ms. Pitcher, had us read and write, and when we got tired we would do arithmetic.

For our class play we put on my favorite scary story, *Little Red Riding Hood.* I wanted to be her, but so did every other girl in the class. We all liked the bright red cape with the fancy hood. Being a good pretender, I knew I could do a fine job skipping through the forest on the way to Grandmother's house.

My second choice was the wolf, but that was every boy in the class's first choice. They all wanted to wear the hairy coat and sneak through the forest trying to trick Red Riding Hood. Being a good pretender, I knew I could do a fine job at that too.

Unfortunately, Ms. Pitcher picked Martina to be Little Red and mistakenly chose Pedro to be the big bad one.

I was sometimes happy for Martina getting to be Red because she was my bestest friend being the bestest character. And Martina was as good at pretending as me . . . almost. But sometimes during practice, watching Martina say, "My, what big eyes you have, Grandma," I got mad inside because . . . well . . . it was exactly what I wanted to be saying. Being mad at Martina made me sad because you shouldn't be mad over your best friend's good luck. So then I was mad-sad.

Watching Pedro stamp and yell around the stage really steamed me because I would have been a *much* better wolfie.

I would lick my lips as I tried to sweet-convince Martina to leave the brown paper path. "Just behind those trees is a meadow filled with beautiful flowers that your old granny would love. Red Riding Hood, you must go pick her a bunch."

Pedro forgot that first line and mumbled the second. Oh boy, did that really get me steamed.

Dad missed the class play, but that was okay, my part wasn't so big. I was the little yellow bush, sitting between two larger brown bushes, and when the pearly-toothed wolfie passed, hunting Red Riding Hood, my papery leaves quivered and shook. The audience laughed and that made me feel that I was a most excellent frightened yellow bush.

I produced long lists of things that Dad missed. He missed soccer on Sunday. I dribbled the ball between two girls, gave a big kick, and scored. At Ike's karate class on Monday, he learned how to high kick. Afterward, he tried to practice on his blocks and hurt his foot. I made the mistake of laughing, which seemed to make it hurt a ton more. At my ballet class on Tuesday, I am getting good at standing on my toes, and the teacher told me so. Dad missed movie night in the den on Friday, in our pj's, cuddled up on the couch under a Grandma Swishback quilt, with bowls of buttered popcorn. We watched mostly silly movies, because Mom said she "needed a good laugh."

Dad missed it all but mostly I just missed him.

"You will make a fine reporter someday," Mom commented after reading one of my longish letters to Dad listing all our activities. I puffed out my chest — this was a big deal since she already was one.

Kangaroo

Being the keeper of my blankie, Katie my kangaroo used to have a lot of responsibility, but with her pouch now empty she was very sad. I felt bad for her, so one night I did the old kangaroo-switcheroo. I snuck a washcloth from the hallway closet, folded it up, and stuffed it in her pouch. She thought it was my scrap of Swishback blankie and became much happier. Kangaroos are not the smartest animals in the world.

* ❋ *

My favorite day was no longer Saturday. Trying to be in charge, I told everyone what to do and when to do it, but being the boss isn't as much fun as it sounds. Especially when you are taking the place of someone who was much better at being the boss than you.

There were few pancake rules followed. Aprons weren't properly tied, measurements were a mishmash, and there were no discussions about the spelling of flour or the funny sound of words like *llama, yogurt,* and *spatula.*

Also there was much "borrowing and lending" of jobs. Ike grabbed the spoon and attempted to drop the batter down. Instead of simple circles perfectly placed he ended up with a mountain of mush that gushed over the sides of the griddle. Need I say that this was yet another amazing example of Ike Sense? And I told him so. He needed to know that unlike the eggs, Dad's rules should not be broken.

Ike stuck his pancake-battered tongue out at me. I wanted to crack him one with my wooden spoon but that wouldn't have gone over well with Mom. It was a Dad rule: The first one who lifted their hand in anger was wrong and would certainly be punished. I could just hear his warning, *Use your words, not your fists.* I swallowed hard, thinking it was a big responsibility being in charge. I had promised him I would be "can-do"; that was my duty.

Mom helped us make pancakes as best she could, but no matter how hard she tried to beat, melt, or flip, the cakes were never too tasty. I guess Swishbacks really don't make perfect pancakes.

Saturday after Saturday they failed to "meet muster," as Dad would say. Once they were burned on the outside, once mushy on the inside, twice they were too salty, and another morning too floury (NOT flowery!), then

too much baking soda — yech! I felt bad for Mom. This was absolutely not her job, but she kept trying. Then a Saturday came when we waited in the kitchen not so excited about another pancake disaster. Mom entered looking like she was still asleep.

"Grandpa McCarther is coming over to take us out to breakfast at Pancake Palace," she said in a sort of asking way.

"Yesssss," essed Ike, who liked the Pancake Palace 'cause he could order pancakes full of chocolate chips.

"Let's get dressed."

Ike raced to his room. I was not as happy. This would never happen if Dad were here. The Pancake Palace was the enemy.

"Go to the Pancake Palace? Sure, if you like hamburger instead of steak, frozen fish sticks instead of fresh fish, tinfoil instead of pure gold!" Dad would instruct the traitor who made that particular suggestion. I had to figure a way to get him back home — fast.

Pancake Palace — I slowly got dressed. The thought of paying double for pancakes that were not even half as good as ours made me want to puke. This was my fault. Dad left me in charge of the routine and the rules and I had . . .

The knock on my door interrupted my thought. Mom slanted her head into my room.

"Hurry, Grandpa will be here any minute."

Grandpa was fun. It would be a little like having a daddy around — but older.

"Esme — I know making the pancakes is your responsibility, and you have been doing a great job. But I need a little break. You know, get out of the house. No dishes to wash kind of thing. You would really be helping me out. Understand?"

I did.

"Maybe we'll convince Grandpa to take us all to a movie after."

Her head disappeared exactly as the chime of the front doorbell appeared. I quickly finished dressing and marched down the stairs to Grandpa's hugs and kisses.

"What are we up to on the old bedzoo?"

"Second time through to Katie my kangaroo," I smiled.

"Still no X?" Grandpa teased, taking my hand and leading us all out to his car.

"No X."

"Hmmm. Too bad. We'll think of something."

I didn't comment on the poor quality of pancakes at the Palace or say a word about our duty to Dad to make pancakes while he was away. I didn't even comment on the flood of syrup Ike poured onto his plate. I was very proud of myself.

"How are your pancakes, dear?"

"Top-dog, Mom," I said, then gulped another cardboardy piece.

I had a duty to make things just a little easier for my mom.

Every day, all the time, she was doing work and chores: writing or making calls for a new *Drum & Bugle* article, cleaning, shopping, cooking, laundrying, walking Napoleon, paying the bills, and double-dealing with Ike, who had more problems and was getting into more trouble "than you could shake a stick at."

One Sunday she even tried to mow the lawn. Ike and I sat on the front stoop watching her pull the rope to the engine over and over. The machine would make sad little whirls and whirrs but then sit silent.

"Dad does it in one pull," Ike challenged.

"Sometimes two," I helpfully called out across the lawn, then suggested, "Maybe it's broken."

Ike and I burst out laughing, knowing it was not.

"It's not funny!" she yelled, and stormed into the house. Later a corporal from the base came and started it with one pull. Ike and I happily sat outside while he back-and-forth-marched the lawn in his fatigues.

Mom was right. It wasn't funny. I could help more. I would help more. I promised to help more. I'd empty the dishwasher, bring my own dirty clothes downstairs, put out my school clothes at night, and not get into any silly arguments with Ike.

Every once in a great while Dad did call us from the great faraway. He couldn't tell us exactly where he was or exactly what he was doing because it was a secret. I imagined him standing in the center of a giant desert. Not another person near, only sand as far as anyone could possibly see, camel looking over his shoulder, phone pressed to his ear. He asked me what I was doing and I said I couldn't exactly tell him because it was a secret too. I wondered if he closed his eyes and imagined me standing in our kitchen, Ike and Mom looking over my shoulder, phone pressed to my ear.

Each call ended with, "Esme, Ike, I love you and soon I'll be home to tell you exactly so."

The nights were difficult because he was not here to tuck me in and I didn't have my blankie to cuddle against my cheek. The days were difficult because that was when you were told bad news. When Principal Pershing poked her partly gray, all-the-way curly head into class we all held our breaths — one girl sent home — one boy sent home. We were all so very brave. It was our duty.

Lamb, Lion

One really windy, cold day, Grandpa took us out to the playground. He said, "Don't worry, March comes in like a lion and goes out like a lamb."

Ike and I thought this was hilarious and laughed so hard we nearly burst, because everyone knows that if a lion is even near a lamb it eats it. The next week Grandpa brought me a cuddly lion and curly lamb. So far, I have to say, lying on my bed together, Larry my lion has been extremely polite to Lucy my lamb.

* ⊙ *

In history class, Ms. Pitcher taught us that a long time ago, in World War II, fought during my great-grandfather's years, the children at home did many things to help the soldiers who were away. She said that this helping was called the "home front" because they did it right here at home in the good ol' U.S. of A. and that it was a very important part of winning the war.

My hand shot up but before Ms. Pitcher could call on

me I burst, "What can we do to help on this 'home front'?"

"Please wait to be called on, Esme."

"Yes, ma'am, but . . ."

"Does anyone have any ideas about what we can do to help?"

I swiveled my head to my classmates. Some were deep-thinking, others confused. Richie and Georgina sat in the back, with bored to pieces expressions, passing notes and not paying much attention, which is what they did best.

Pedro, who had taken my second-choice part in the play, piped in, "At my house before we go to sleep we pray for all the soldiers' safe return."

"Good, Pedro. That is something. What else? Something more . . ."

The lunch bell rang a sudden end to the discussion. Richie and Georgina, no longer bored to pieces, brown lunch bags clasped in hands, led the class's hungry charge from the room.

Sitting on the seesaw at recess up and downing across from Martina, it began bothering me. We weren't doing anything to help on our home front except worrying, and I wasn't sure that really helped at all.

"What do you think about the home front?" I questioned up the slanted wood.

"I liked it better when we were learning about the Minutemen. In a minute they would rush out of their houses and hide in the woods to get them lobster-backs . . . lobsterbacks!" Martina giggled, straightened her legs, and launched me back down.

My imagination drifted off to lines of live lobsters marching through the dirt streets, claws gripping mus-kets, antennae sticking out of pointy red hats. Then I thought of the children during the World War help-ing the soldiers on the home front. We weren't doing anything. . . .

"Let me down, Esme," Martina moaned from the up-side of the seesaw, but I was thinking so hard I didn't hear a word and didn't budge.

"Let me down! Esme!" Martina cried. But my mind was in another country.

"Esmerelda Swishback McCarther!" commanded Prin-cipal Pershing from near the swings. "You let her down this minute!"

And being a good soldier, I did. Martina hit hard. There was crying. We ended up in the school office, sit-ting on the pen-scarred wooden bench under the kin-dergarten's rows of blue construction paper pictures. "It was an accident, I swear. I would never do anything to hurt you. I am sorry," I apologized. Which was totally true, so although Martina's bottom was still sore, she nodded that she believed me, and although Principal

Pershing was still totally sore, she nodded and believed me too.

"Back to class, you two."

"But . . ."

Before our principal could turn and retreat into her office I explained what we had learned in class and asked, "What can we do to help on our home front?"

I flashed a hopeful look at Martina. Someone in such a principal position would have an easy solution to this hard home front problem.

"All do what they can," she commented, "and there's not much we *can* do."

My stomach felt like the trapeze artist who just missed grabbing her partner's hands. It flipped and flopped, tumbling down toward my feet.

Martina stopped sobbing, screwed up her face, and stated, "My mom says in the marines there is always *something* we can do."

I felt that Martina would one day make a top-dog marine.

Monkey, Muskrat

Martina gave me my monkey. One rainy playdate she pulled it from her backpack and placed it onto my bed-zoo, sliding it between Mandrake my scruffy-whiskered muskrat and Lucy my snowy-haired lamb.

"I don't have any animals with X to give you but I was wondering if you had room for another M?"

"Sure I do. Thanks."

"My great-aunt Joan gave it to me."

I calm-waited for the rest of the story, since no one gave away a perfectly good monkey, even to a best friend.

"I named it after her husband, who she doesn't like so much anymore. And if she doesn't like him anymore, neither do I."

"Oh."

"It reminds me of him. If you could not change his first name it would probably make him feel better. The thing is, it doesn't start with an M. It's Karl, with a K."

She was worried that since the monkey's first name did not start with the same letter as his last name (monkey), like my other animals, it might get teased.

"The others will treat him like their best friend no matter what his name is. And look . . ."

I picked Karl up from between Mandrake and Lucy and moved him exactly one spot over to the right.

"See, now he sits next to my nightingale — Florence."

This showed Martina that there would be no teasing on my bed and that her monkey would be in good company.

So that is how I adopted Karl the monkey.

* ❋ ⊛ ❋ *

My hand was already up as Ms. Pitcher turned from the blackboard where she had just pink-chalk-written 4 x 4 = ____.

"Esme?"

"We didn't finish talking about what we can do to help on our home front."

"It's math, not history," whined Georgina, who paid just as little attention to one as to the other.

"Shhhh," growled Martina in a way that made Georgina sink deep into her chair, cross her arms, and look down.

Math is my favorite subject, but this was more important than worrying about favorites.

"That is true, Georgina, but this is important," agreed our teacher as if she were reading my mind. "Let's take a few minutes to finish. Suggestions?"

Whew, do I like Ms. Pitcher. To make sure the pouting Georgina got the message loud and clear Martina continued to stare at her. Whew, do I like Martina.

Hands shot up, whispered ideas crisscrossed desks, and shouted suggestions bounced off the blackboard, followed by the stern "Wait your turn, children." There were so many ideas that Ms. Pitcher had to erase 1 x 1 = ____, 2 x 2 = ____, 3 x 3 = ____ and the recently written 4 x 4 = ____ to write them all down. The board was chock-full of suggestions that went from the kooky and crazy ("We should fly over there and drop candy.") to the possible, doable, but not really helpful ("We should draw pictures and write letters."). After a trillion ideas, the exhausted class went silent.

"We will just be in the way," barked Richie, eyes narrowed and arms folded, chin stubbornly pasted down on his neck. He looked like one of those flat-headed angry dogs that Dad always told us to stay clear of. Martina moved her head slightly right so Richie could just barely see the whites of her eyes. He choked on his next sentence, not letting it fully leave his mouth. It sounded like a turkey gobble. Everyone laughed.

"Class," called Ms. Pitcher to quiet us.

The thought of not doing anything made my body feel like a pirate's spyglass collapsing down, until it was small enough to fit in a pocket. "We'll vote. That's the democratic thing to do," decided Ms. Pitcher.

"Yes, the democratic thing," repeated Martina, her eyeballs still cruelly shifted toward Richie.

"Absolutely demm-ooo-crat-tic," I drawled slowly. I wasn't exactly sure what it meant we would do but knew that it was better than big Richie's and little Georgina's bitter frowns.

"Raise your hands if you want to do something to help."

I held my breath, raised my hand, and closed my eyes. As if in a deep sleep I could barely hear Ms. Pitcher's voice counting, 1, 2, 3, 4, 5. . . . I couldn't keep my eyes closed and my breath held any longer — breathe — open — so many hands were raised!

We voted (which *was* "the democratic thing to do"), and decided 23–2 (you can guess who the two were) that we would, just like the children of World War II, do many things on the home front over here to help our fathers, mothers, brothers, sisters, and friends over there.

I was so proud of my class . . . and Martina . . . and my teacher . . . and myself.

Nightingale

Mom's first cousin, Curtis, stayed with us in Frankfurt for a week and gave me my little baby blue nightingale. Until Karl the monkey arrived, this bird was the single exception to my rule of making my stuffed animals' first names start with the same letter as their last. I couldn't resist naming her Florence after a famous nurse I had read a picture book about.

* ✿ *

Ms. Pitcher explained that just like in World War II, gasoline was very important, and that every gallon of it we saved meant the soldiers might return home one precious minute sooner.

Those of us who could, rode our bicycles to school so our parents didn't have to drive us. Ike and I had to get up a full thirty minutes earlier so we would not be late. But we were so happy that we were helping that it didn't matter one *eye-o-tah* (which was a word Mom used that meant "not even a little bit"). We would glide down our driveway and sharp-turn up our street, and as we hard-pumped, others would fall in behind. With a tail of ten kids, including Pedro and Bridget, we neared midway, and we didn't have to slow down even a bit as Martina fell in on her banana seat, pink-tasseled handlebarred bike and delivered a big "Ooooh Raaaah!" which is Marine talk for "I am here and happy about it."

A block later, Ike's friend Stony Jackson would rip down his steep driveway and pedal alongside Ike, yackety-yakking until a car would come and he would have to grudgingly fall in behind my brother. Once the car passed, Stony would double-pedal-pump and catch up to Ike to continue their chatter. When our troop of kids turned into the school parking lot, Ms. Pitcher and several other teachers would welcome us with applause and help us lock up our bikes. I loved helping on the home front because it made me feel like I was part of the good ol' U.S. of A, which made me feel like I was part of the army, which made me feel like I was part of my dad.

Every day in every way we careful-conserved. Four people in a car, lights off when you left a room, and when it got cold we wore sweaters inside instead of turning up the heat. It was simple math: if we collected enough saved seconds, they would grow into minutes, the minutes would grow into hours, and the hours into days, and then soon our parents would be on their way home.

*   *   *

We combed our brains and searched our textbooks to find other ways to help our home front.

Bridget, whose brother was in the navy, suggested going door-to-door selling war bonds to our neighbors like they did in World War II, to help buy things for the fight. But when we asked Bridget's uncle who worked downtown at the savings and loan bank, we found there were no bonds to sell, which was okay since we didn't know exactly what they were anyway.

Arthur, whose dad was in the air force, read in a book that many families grew "victory gardens" in their yards. They would grow vegetables so that the soldiers had plenty. I thought it would be a good idea if we didn't eat any of our vegetables so the soldiers would have more. No more broccoli, green beans, or spinach for us! Ms. Pitcher didn't think that was such a good idea. So, after school we went over to Arthur's house, dragged shovels from the garage, and tried to dig up the backyard to plant all sorts of seeds, from corn to zucchini, every vegetable except for peas, since Martina thought they tasted like little green boogers.

The dirt was frozen solid. No matter how hard we hit the shovels down, they just clanged on the ground. We all agreed it was best to wait for the spring to start our "victory garden."

*   *   *

Martina, who had thought about our problem for many an hour, suggested that like the children did during World War II, we should have a scrap metal drive. Scrap metal is any piece of metal that is garbage here but can be melted down and shaped into armor to protect our mothers, fathers, sisters, brothers, and friends over there.

"We can't do that," moaned Pedro, "we're too small."

Martina turned to her side, made a big muscle, and stated in no uncertain terms, "We can do it!"

And so we did.

Octopus

An octopus has eight arms that all work together. Ollie my octopus has only seven, since for no good reason Napoleon chewed one off. A sevetopus? Was I mad? You bet!

✳ ❂ ✳

That next Sunday was the Abraham Lincoln Elementary School's very first scrap metal drive. Martina and I dragged our wagons up Concord Court and down Sumter Street, past Flanders Way and across Lexington Avenue, collecting any rusted old remains. We found seventeen empty food cans, a hubcap, six pieces of pipe, and many parts that came from machines that we could not identify.

On the corner of Gold and Juno Streets we hit the jackpot.

"Look!" squealed Martina.

"Oh, my! It's huge. This will protect, like, a whole army."

Squatting on the curb like a giant rusted accordion

was an abandoned radiator. We eased our wagon alongside. Martina went to one end and I to the other.

"One," she started.

"Two," I added.

"THREE!!" we yelled, and lifted. It didn't move one inch.

We counted again and then again, switched sides, bent our knees, used our heads, but no matter how hard we pushed or pulled it wouldn't budge. Resting on the curb, we did not admit defeat. Instead, we decided to return with help to collect this great iron prize. We took a deep breath, let out a big "Ooooh Raaah!" and continued on our metal collecting way.

"It's too bad we don't need plastic, " observed Martina as we headed home. We had come across tons of garbage made of plastic.

"Or single shoes," I added, because as we dragged our wagon here and there, we came across many scrumpled old solitary shoes, boots, and sneakers lying lonely in the gutter.

"I wonder why there is always only one and never a pair," questioned Martina.

"Weird . . . maybe a pirate captain with a peg leg lives around here." I limped along.

"Could be, could be . . ." Martina giggled. "Or maybe a flamingo who doesn't like to get her pants dirty."

She stopped and bird-posed, putting her left foot on her right knee and her hands under her armpits.

I shrieked.

We dragged our clattering junk down the streets, making up hilarious single shoe stories. As we broke the early Sunday morning silence, curtains slow-rose, doors slammed, and car engines started — we had woken our neighbors from their sleep.

At the center of our dead-end street, we dumped our collected junk. Soon other classmates turned the corner with their overflowing carts.

"Did you guys come up with any good single shoe stories?" Martina wondered.

Our friends stopped laughing and stared at us as if we had just landed from a faraway planet.

"What kind of stories?" asked Bridget.

"Never mind."

Our tangled pile of rusted metal grew as each wagon was unloaded.

"It looks like museum art," said my mom, admiring the collection.

Together, Martina's and my head cocked to the side, like Napoleon's when he hears a strange sound. It didn't look anything like art to me — it looked exactly like a pile of junk.

Our neighbors noticed this super start and pitched

in. They emptied their houses of useless metal and added it to our huge collection. Soon many broken machines, tangled hangers, and boxes of dented cans were brought and piled high. Several people mentioned that it was an extremely patriotic thing we were doing. We held our chins to the sky, proud of our work.

Ancient Mrs. Wood, widowed once in the Great War, and then again in the next, pushed a misplaced car fender four blocks in her shopping cart.

"Bella," my mother cautioned, "you shouldn't have done that."

"All for a good cause," she cracked smartly. Then with her long ringed fingers creaking under the strain, she pried open a large tin of her famous homemade gingersnaps. The price we paid for taking one or two of these circular treats was to listen to her tales about the way times used to be. It wasn't too high a price because the snaps were A-number-one — and so were her stories.

She had crossed our country from the Empire State Building to the Grand Canyon and traveled this earth from the pyramids of Egypt to the Great Wall of China and met all sorts of strange and wonderful people along the way.

"I have sat down and broken bread with kings and

criminals," she elegantly explained, her silver-frosted curls wobbling as she nodded.

"Once while traveling to Tombouctou I was wooed by a quite handsome prince of the desert. If I had married that gentleman, I can assure you I would not be sitting on a curb in Alexandria, Virginia, eating gingersnaps with you girls. I can tell you that. No, indeed, I would be sitting on a jeweled throne, the queen of all the lands stretching from Tombouctou, on through Tomboucthree to the mountains past Tomboucsix!"

Martina and I smiled, wondering how fun it would be to have her on top of the playground jungle gym for our imaginary games.

Mrs. Wood sucked in her powdered cheeks and described how heroically handsome her husband had looked in his doughboy uniform.

"Doughnut uniform?" asked Ike, thinking that after devouring three gingersnaps he was going to get something else to eat.

"Doughboys were what they called the soldiers of the first war. I do not know why," she said. "Maybe you could look that up for me, Isaac. The *why* of doughboys."

Ike winced at her use of his full-out first name — maybe because he didn't like it, maybe because the last time he heard it was when Dad told us he was going away. He mumbled in that Ike way when someone gave him work he didn't want to do.

*   *   *

Mrs. Wood didn't comment on the mumble. The slack skin around her faded gray eyes folded as she squinted into the distance. It was as if our street did not end in a curbed circle ten yards from where we sat cross-legged, but extended out in a straight line for miles and miles toward the afternoon's falling sun, and she could see her "doughboy" as clearly, right then and there, as if he were marching home to her in the real here and now.

"That was the war to end all wars," she commented to no one in particular.

When Mrs. Wood was done telling about her terrific travels and we were done devouring her terrific snaps, she shook her head, pressed her tongue against the roof of her mouth, and made an amazed clucking sound. Then, with a girlish giggle, she tossed the empty cookie tin into our metallic mound, leaned on her cart for support, and wheeled away.

Martina's and my smile did not last long. The single most nastiest man on the block, Mr. Wormser, who kept each and every baseball accidentally batted into his bushes and promised to pull off our noses if we ever set one foot on his property, came shuffling toward us. His cane kicking out, his crooked smile pulled to one side of his lightbulb-like bald head, he held tightly in his bony hand one single bent fork.

"Oh, my goodness gracious!" he crazy-croaked at our pile. "You children just remember it is easier to get into something than to get out of it."

"Yes, sir," Pedro and Ike dutifully responded to the grouch, respecting their elders even though what he said made less sense than Ike Sense at its worst.

"Fustilug" slipped out. Martina looked at me with a big question mark written across her face. But before I could erase it, Mom glanced at me with a sharp warning look that quickly slow-melted into a knowing smile that made me feel warm inside.

Mr. Wormser turned his slanted face toward Martina and me, cleared his throat with a big attention-getting "AHEM," and adjusted his thin round eyeglasses as if he were trying to get us into crisp clear focus.

"You're welcome."

He testily chucked his fork on top of our mountain of scrap. It made a lonely triangle-like tinkle as it found its way to the very bottom of our pile. As he crankily caned away, we silent-hoped he wouldn't look or come back.

"All do what they can, children," commented Ms. Pitcher, echoing our principal, and then to try and make us better understand added, "You work with the neighbors you have. They're not always the neighbors you might want or wish to have." Then she shrugged as if to tell us that in the case of Mr. Wormser there was absolutely positively nothing we could do.

Pig, Python

One day we drove to a carnival in Fredricksburg. There were crazy upside-down and sideways rides like you wouldn't believe, cotton candy in three different colors, crazy clowns, and many strange games. Dad's favorite game was a giant-giant hammer.

"Step right up and test your strength!" the man leaning on the hammer like it was a cane yelled. My dad handed him a dollar and he was given the giant-giant hammer. He spit on his hands, which was kind of gross, swung the hammer behind his head and then down. It smashed the baby seesaw, sending the square rocketing up. It hit the bell hard. Everyone oohed and aahed. He hit it twice and the man who owned the giant-giant hammer gave me my choice of prizes. That is how Polly my potbelly pig and Pete my python came to live in my bedzoo.

* ⚙ *

Our scrap metal drive was a sensational success.

Martina and I and all our classmates (except for Richie and Georgina who hadn't participated one bit) were pictured on the front page of the *Drum & Bugle,* next to our giant pile of parts, with Principal Pershing pinning red, white, and blue ribbons on us. The story, written by my mother, told it exactly like it had happened except for the part about cranky old Mr. Wormser forking over one lousy fork and some scrambled egg advice. She said it was "common courtesy" to leave that out.

"I have written many articles for the *Drum & Bugle,* interviewed generals and colonels, and I even once spoke to a president, but this is by far the article I am the most delighted to have written," she remarked as she careful-clipped around its edges. With her wedding ring hand, she smoothed the clear photo album cellophane over the article. Then, arm in arm, we read together, her pointer underlining each word.

Children Collect Scrap to Help War Effort

By Penelope Swishback McCarther

Alexandria, Virginia — Ms. Molly Pitcher's 2nd-grade class at Abraham Lincoln Elementary School held a scrap metal drive to aid the war effort and to show support for our troops fighting abroad.

Early Sunday morning, the children scoured the neighborhood, collecting all manner of metal in their wagons, then deposited it at the center of Saratoga

Road. Many neighbors, friends, and family members pitched in to help and by day's end a huge pile of forks, tin cans, hangers, rusted car parts, radiators, and even an old oven had been brought to the cul-de-sac for pickup.

"What's that?"
"A cul-de-sac? It's when a street ends in a big round circle. Like our street."
Ike nodded.
"Here's my favorite part."

"We want to help out on the home front so our friends and family can return from the war as soon as possible," stated Esmerelda Swishback McCarther, one of the student leaders of the scrap drive, whose father is in the middle of his tour of duty.

"Can we send a copy to Dad?"
"His whole unit, every man and woman, private to major, will have a copy of the *Drum & Bugle* by Tuesday."

"We hope," added Ms. Pitcher, "the scrap metal will be melted down and turned into armor to protect our troops."

As the sun set, it made the enormous mound of metal glow orange and red. A truck from the army arrived, loaded the scrap, and headed back to the base.

"We are grateful for any and all support we get from the home front, where every citizen can be a soldier. Anything done here helps us defeat our enemies over there," commented Captain Capra of the U.S. Office of War Information.

For their patriotism and hard work, each child received a red, white, and blue battle ribbon from their principal, Ms. Jacqueline Pershing, and a certificate of commendation from the army for a job well done.

"So what do you think?"

I wore a big ear-to-ear grin. "You sure know how to tell a story."

Which made Mom put on the same grin. She got up from my bed and started to pluck the week's dirty clothes from the hamper that hung from my closet door.

"I have to get the laundry in ASAP." Which is army talk for "As Soon As Possible." I jumped up to help pick the clothes off the floor.

"Thank you, young lady. Fish sticks tonight?"

"My favorite."

"And spaghetti?"

"No sauce," I reminded.

Loaded with an armful of smelly socks, I followed my mom down to the basement washing machine.

Queen Bee

Queenie is black and yellow, with a fuzzy big bottom and two floppy wings made out of lace. My mom gave her to me for Ike's first birthday. It was the only time I ever got a present for someone else's birthday. Dad sometimes calls Mom the queen bee, which is kind of funny since she does not have a black-and-yellow fuzzy big bottom.

* ◎ *

"Esme, *so* many soldiers slap me on the back to say, 'Tell your daughter thanks,' that I am black-and-blue and proud all over!" my dad joked when he next called from his base. "Everyone has a copy of the paper and I am bursting with pride."

The phone static crackled.

"I folded it up and keep it in my top pocket next to a picture of the three of you."

"Which part did you like the best?"

"The picture. You look so big."

"Where are you?" I asked.

"It's a secret. Where are you?"

"In the good ol' U.S. of A.," I chirped cheerfully, not feeling the need to keep secrets from him any longer. Sharing that not-so-secret secret made him very happy, which made me very happy.

"That, my girl, is a good place to be. A good place to be . . . ," he repeated, or the phone echoed a bad connection.

"Ike around? Ike around?"

"Ike! It's Dad!" I yelled.

He charged up the stairs from the basement and grabbed the phone.

"Hello. Dad? Dad? Hello?" He dropped the phone; it rebounded off the floor, swung from its cord, and clattered across the kitchen cabinets. Ike stormed away, back to the basement.

"That's not funny, Esme!"

I caught the still bouncing phone and put it to my ear.

"Dad?" My own voice bounced back to me. "Dad?"

I hung up and stood thinking. Mom entered.

"What happened?'

"We were disconnected."

"Oh. That's too bad. He'll call back when he can." She continued to the stove. "Why don't you finish your homework and then we'll have dinner."

Nodding, I headed toward my room. As I passed the

open basement door, I stopped and listened. Ike rumbled his trucks along the floor, talking to them, pretending they were people. I clomped down the stairs to give him fair warning of my arrival. He stopped his imaginary trucking and stared up at me.

"You know, Dad *was* on the phone. We just got disconnected."

"I know."

"He'll call back when he can."

"I know."

"Next time you can talk first."

He ducked his head and went back to pushing his long-necked crane. I squatted down to a laddered fire engine and gently rolled it back and forth. Ike didn't bite my head off so I eased down to a full sit and moved the bright red truck farther along the carpet. There was a long silence as we both pushed our separate trucks across the floor. I hadn't ever played with Ike's toys before. He never let me and I never wanted to. We both needed time to figure out exactly what we were supposed to do.

With his dirty brown buzz cut, sharp blue eyes, and jaw that came out past a flat forehead, Ike looked a lot like Dad — only smaller.

"There's a fire over there."

He pointed at a block-built building at the edge where the carpet met the concrete.

I stuttered out a low vibrating siren sound and rumbled the truck toward the pretend blaze. He grabbed his big red pumper with his left hand and the small fire chief's car with his right and raced them past me.

"Faster, Esme! Faster! We have to save the people."

Rhinoceros Ofcourserous

Anytime I say "rhinoceros," my dad says "ofcourserous."

"This is Reginald my rhinoceros."

"Ofcourserous! Glad to make your acquaintance."

He says he didn't make the word ofcourserous *up, and that it is from a famous movie. But he can't remember which one. I don't believe him. I think he made it up and doesn't want to admit it because it is sillier than spatula. Ofcourserous.*

* ❁ *

In math class, while others learned to add and then subtract, subtract and then add, I watched the wall clock's thin black second hand collect minutes on its march toward dismissal. Even though it is my favorite subject, I couldn't help but drift away, thinking about the next slice of my dad's one hundred day and ninety-nine night tour of duty. "Doodee," I muttered Ike's mangled pronunciation, and grinned. Tour, not such a funny word, but then I imagined it as an *actual* tour. Dad sitting in a bus, driving across the desert; the guide gripping the microphone close to her lips, pointing out places of interest, like when we went on the class trip to Colonial Williamsburg.

"If you look out the right side of the bus you will see an excellent example of sand," explained the peppy tour guide. "And if you look out the window on your left you will see . . . more sand!"

I chuckled out loud at the thought.

"Esmerelda . . . Esmerelda McCarther."

I looked up and swallowed my smile whole. Standing at the door was Principal Pershing calling out my whole first name and sometimes my last name in front of the whole class.

"Esmerelda. Esmerelda McCarther . . . Esmerelda. Esmerelda McCarther . . ."

How long had she been standing there? Did she know I wasn't listening to the tower of tens that Ms. Pitcher properly summed up? How many times had she called my name? I wanted to crawl into my desk and hide behind the ruler, but being too big for that . . .

"Esmerelda, a moment," she inchwormed her pointer at me, requesting my immediate attention.

Slow-rising from my seat, I winced in pain at her continued use of my extended first name. Then I wondered *why* and then worried *why* I was being called out of class ten minutes before school was over. Everyone's eyes grabbed at me, trying to hold me down, but the pull of that inchworming principal's finger was just too strong. I zigzagged through the desks toward the door and halfway there I thought of why and my knees started to shake. Not me. Please not me. Each class-mate I passed looked down at their doodle-filled note-book, as if, like the flu, they could catch whatever the principal was going to give to me. Not me. Please not me. Martina smiled lightly and gave me the ol' thumbs-up as I exited.

"Your brother is in my office," stated the principal plainly when we stepped out into the hall.

"Ike?" I asked for no particular reason but to fill up the empty hallway air. I didn't have another brother. Ike it was.

"He has had a bad day. A scuffle in the yard."

My knees gradually stopped their crazy rhythms. My stomach stopped doing gymnastic tumbles and the corners of my mouth turned up away from frown toward a sky-high smile. It wasn't my nightly night-mare become real in the day. It was okay — only Ike, in a "scuffle."

"There is nothing funny about a fight, young lady."

"No, ma'am. I'm sure Ike didn't start . . ."

But she was down the hall before I could finish.

In the main office, Ike was perched at the edge of that very same pencil-scarred wooden bench that ran along the faded blue construction-papered bulletin board. The left knee of his pants was ripped and his angry face was finger-painted with streaks of dirty tears.

"What happened?"

"I got into a fight with Stony, he . . ."

"This way, you two."

Principal Pershing swung open the heavy wooden door that bore her gold-plaqued name and title. We climbed into the two heavy wooden chairs and stared across the wide expanse of the cluttered, heavy wooden desk at our principal's creased face.

"Isaac, would you care to tell your sister what happened?"

"He said he was going to hit me. . . ."

Stony and Ike had a history, so the idea that they had an argument did not surprise me. They were what Mom called "light-switch friends" — on again, off again. When they were on they were "thick as a brick and as sweet as honey," and when they were off . . . But a fist-fight . . . Ike, even though his curious Ike Sense often guided his actions, wasn't like that at all.

"He's half your size," I pointed out.

". . . with a stick. He said he was going to hit me with a stick . . . a big one," he added, and stressed the "big" to help excuse his actions.

I looked up to see if the "big stick" story held any water with the principal. Not even a teaspoon.

"Did he hit you with the stick?" she quietly queried.

I swiveled back to Ike, almost hoping. He sad-shook his head.

"Did he even have a stick?" she calm-continued.

"Not that I saw . . . no, but he said . . ."

Having barely one leg to stand on, his hurt voice limped away. Ike had hit a kid in the playground who was half his size because the kid had threatened to hit him with a stick. This was Ike Sense at its worst! The bell rang, interrupting Ms. Pershing and releasing our classmates for the day. Her mouth twisted in impatient knots as she waited for the clanging to finish, and when it did the lecture began.

"Now, I know that your father is away and that is very hard. But, Isaac Ulysses Swishback McCarther . . ."

Oh, gosh, she used his middle name. I panicked inside, wondering if he would be suspended, kicked out of school, or worse. . . .

"Today you have broken many school rules and I'm not really sure what to do with you."

She paused and took in a deep noisy breath through her banana-curved nose.

"I would prefer not to worry your mom about this. Is this something you two can solve?" Both our heads bobbed like Halloween apples in a tub.

"Good. Isaac — do I have your word that this will not happen again?"

Ike's head continued to bob.

"Even if next time Stony Jackson says he is going to hit you with a tree trunk?"

The bob slowed as he thought of Stony trying to swing a tree trunk at him.

"Then on your way, you two."

Signaling that she was done with us, she steep-curled her nose down, pretending to examine a stack of papers. We thanked her, and as we backed out, I assured her that I would talk some sense into Ike, even though I knew that was fairly impossible.

Squirrel

Mom says when I saw Sylvester in the toy store window it was love at first sight. I bought my squirrel with my very own money. I saved my allowance and when I reached $10.99, which is as close to eleven dollars as you can come before it actually becomes eleven dollars, I opened my little safe (the combination is a secret), took the money to the toy store, and bought Sylvester my squirrel. At the last minute, Mom had to chip in seventy-nine more cents because they charged me something called tax, which I did not think was very fair. Still, I was very proud of myself.

* ⊙ *

Silent as fish, we traveled the hall upstream into the rush of students heading home. Still silent, we passed the playground where the day's trouble had begun. Children raced around the swings, monkey bars, and see-saw. There was no trace of the afternoon's fight. We walked all the way to the mailbox on the corner of Normandy Avenue before Ike begged, "Esme . . . say something."

I considered what Mom would say in this sort of situation but then just said what I had to say.

"Dad's rules are all we have until he comes back. You absolutely broke his playground rules."

"I know it . . . I just wasn't thinking. . . ."

"That's Ike Sense, all right — just not thinking."

I shouldn't have said that, but I did. His shoulders folded down low as if I had just punched his stomach. I felt pretty bad. I had been a fustilug, but he had broken at least one, if not more, of the playground rules that Dad had drilled into us.

1. Wait your turn.

2. Don't talk to adult strangers.

3. Don't throw sand.

4. Don't leave the playground without telling an adult.

5. The first person who hits is always wrong.

"Number five," I said matter-of-factly.

"Five," agreed Ike as he fought hard to hold back tears.

"Sticks and stones . . ."

"I know . . . I know . . . ," moaned Ike. "Sticks and stones may break my bones, but names . . ."

". . . and dopey threats will never harm me," I finished.

Sticks and stones was a no-brainer. Thoughtless fustilugs would talk and say hurtful things, but that was never a reason to hit.

According to Dad, "The first person who hits is the first person to run out of good ideas, and a McCarther never runs out of good ideas." Dad was big on rules. Rules were important. After all, in the army you had more rules "than you could shake a stick at."

My father, Sergeant August Aloysius McCarther the Third, has made it super clear that you don't want to go and break his rules.

"I didn't want to break his rules."

"I know you didn't, Ike."

"It's my duty not to . . . ," Ike muttered sadly and proudly at the same exact time.

I chewed that over, then nodded in agreement. While Dad was away it was our duty to follow his rules.

"I broke my duty. . . ."

The image of Ike breaking his "doodee" almost made me break out laughing, but the sad trickle of tears that slid down into his furred brown coat collar stopped me.

We turned onto our street. The dogwood trees, with yellow ribbons tied to their trunks in hopes of our soldiers' safe return, stood at attention as we passed. Our house squatted on the far corner. The white paint had started to potato-peel off parts of the walls. Dad would fix that when he got back. He'd take us to the hardware store to buy paint and turpentine.

Turpentine! Dad thought *turpentine* was a funnier word than *yogurt, llama,* or even *spatula.*

"You going to tell Mom?"

"Turpentine."

I didn't mean to say that; the silly word just slipped from my lips. Ike looked up at me, scrunched his damp face in confusion, and then for the first time since I saw him sitting on that bench in the office, smiled. Somehow, at that moment, "turpentine" was the very best thing to say. Funny, how you can get lucky that way. Then Ike's smile just as quickly disappeared.

"What about Daddy?"

What about Daddy? I repeated inside my head. For the first time since my father had left for war, I was angry with him. How could I possibly be angry with him when he wasn't even here? The house needed painting, Ike got into a fight, Mom needed help, and we hadn't had a good pancake in weeks. He had other duties — duties here with us. Which came first, the sergeant or the daddy? My lips went straight and my teeth gritted hard together at this dangerous thought. I knew deep inside that even thinking this I had somehow broken an important rule. I sucked in a deep breath of cool air through my nose and looked down at Ike, who waited, expectant eyes, chin raised, for my answer to "What about Daddy?" *Think, Esme, think what to say. Be owl wise.* But at that moment I was so mad-sad about so

many things that I had gone blank inside my head and couldn't put any words in any correct order.

I stepped over the curb onto the faded stone walk that led to the house. From behind the front door you could barely hear Napoleon's muffled welcoming barks.

"I miss Dad," I soft-said. It wasn't something I had ever said since he had left. But now, having said it, I felt like I had broken another big rule.

"Me too."

Ike slipped his hand into mine and squeezed. We continued up the path toward home.

Tiger, Turtle

This is my third time through the T's. I started with Tina my tiger, which I got from Mommy's little brother, Tom, when he visited us in Germany two years ago. He took us on an amazing boat trip down the blue Danube, a river in Germany whose banks are dotted with ancient castles that Tom told us are ruled by ferocious trolls. (Tom likes telling stories so I am not sure how true that part is.)

My turtle's name is Tililah, which Ike insists is no name at all. This is another case of Ike Sense. Since my turtle is named Tililah, it is most definitely a name. When we first arrived in Alexandria, Delilah, a corporal lady in my dad's division, gave me Tililah. She explained that this turtle would always remind me that "slow and steady wins the race." Even though I like Delilah and Tililah very much, I don't believe that one bit because anytime we race in gym I have noticed that the fastest one wins and the slowest, steady one does not. Sometimes grown-ups don't know very much about kids.

* ✿ *

I bounced on my bed, examining my crossed-off calendar. It looked like I was X in a very long tic-tac-toe game that I should have won at least ten days ago. To try and make the game a tie, I decided to circle the rest of the days Dad was gone. With my thick black marker I circled day seventy-two, a sunny Sunday. At least I had Grandpa McCarther's visit to look forward to.

Napoleon's happy howls from the living room announced Grandpa's arrival. I tucked Tililah back into my bedzoo between Sylvester my squirrel and Tina my tiger, jumped off the bed, and raced out of my room, almost knocking Ike down the stairs.

When Grandpa saw us he gave us a big double hug. His eyes were not quite as bright sky blue, his hair more grayed than light brown, his face more gentle, but Grandpa McCarther looked a lot like Daddy, which, when you think about it, is really no great surprise. Crossing the crumbly skin on his arm were the rusty remains of his robin redbreast tattoo, now a faded red-and-black blur.

I looked down at my slender splinter of an arm and knew for certain that that picture could never fit. When

I looked back up, Grandpa was smiling at me in that way grandparents do when they know exactly what you were just thinking. He winked at me to signal that we had just shared the same thought.

"Did you bring me a present, Grandpa?" Ike asked rudely. Grandpa always did bring us something, but it was best left as a surprise and not something expected.

"Isaac!" warned Mom.

"I most certainly did."

He reached behind the couch and slid a wrapped box to Ike, who ripped it open to reveal a hulking yellow dump truck.

"Wow! Thanks, Grandpa."

Ike sped to the basement to test it out with the rest of his collection.

"Esme, I think I have solved quite a prickly problem you have been having." An oddly shaped, awkwardly wrapped package appeared in front of me. Grandpa McCarther was a great solver of prickly problems.

I carefully picked at the taped paper corners and slid the contents out, revealing a big-beaked stuffed bird.

"Esme, dear, finally this is it. This is the X for your bedzoo."

I still had no X. Everyone knows there are very few words that start with that terribly troublesome letter, and absolutely no animals.

"It is a bird, Grandpa, and bird starts with a B, like bandicoot or beetle."

"It is not just any bird, Esme . . . it is a *dodo* bird."

I was silent while my brain raced through the alphabet once, then twice. Both times dodo started with D. But Grandpa was very smart and he would never mistake the D in dodo for the ever-troublesome X, so I checked a third time, because as Dad always said, "three strikes and you are out."

"D — dodo definitely begins with D, not X," I gently reminded him, and then thought, *Grandpa, yer out!*

"Ahhh."

That big open-mouth sound meant Grandpa McCarther had somehow tricked me.

"Dodos are X-tinct, and X-tinct begins with X!"

I threw my arms around his neck to show him how much I loved the gift, then ran upstairs to my bedzoo to name my X-tinct Dodo.

"Hurry back," Grandpa called. Then ordering and asking at the same time, he added, "What say we give you two tykes a little break from your mom and take a park adventure?"

I didn't need a break from Mom, but maybe she needed a break from us.

Unicorn

Unicorns are not real live animals. This has been told to me many times. They are made up, like mermaids, dragons, and werewolves. But if, with a wave of a magic wand, there was one animal I could make real, it would be my unicorn, Ulrich. I can close my eyes and imagine his shiny white coat, long twisty horn straight to the sky, silver hooves kicking up dirt, and me on his back riding through the forest.

* ✪ *

It was a great day with Grandpa. We rode the carousel six times straight — a McCarther family record. I went on the camel, donkey, giraffe, dragon, skipped the elephant because its seat was broken, and finished with two straight rides on the sea horse. We drank dark soda, ate big salt pretzels, three candy bars, a lolly, and a soft vanilla-chocolate-swirled ice-cream cone — having all in the same afternoon was another McCarther family first.

As I held Grandpa's right hand and Ike his left, we walked through the park answering his questions about how school was and what our favorite subjects were.

"Math. Math is my favorite. I like the way everything comes out exactly right in the end."

"That was your father's favorite. . . ."

"Lunch!" spit Ike, blowing rainbow sprinkles off his ice cream. "I like the way everything is always eaten in the end."

"Hmm. Well, if I remember correctly, that was your father's favorite also."

"Grandpa," I cautioned, "he couldn't have had two favorites. Which was it? Math or lunch?"

Ike's face scrunched, preparing to howl in victory. In his mind there was no possible way he could lose this lopsided competition between math and lunch. Tired from watching us on the carousel, Grandpa eased us down onto a wooden slatted bench that overlooked the carved green-and-brown baseball fields where boys and girls batted and caught.

"Why couldn't he? I have two favorites," he glanced at each of us.

Partially satisfied with a tie, Ike relaxed his jaw and attacked his now-soupy ice cream. I smiled at Grandpa's skill at escaping this trap. The smack of a bat hitting a ball and calls of "Out!" and "Safe!" made us look out onto the ball field.

"Grandpa, do all Dads come back from war?"

"No, Ike, they don't."

It was late afternoon and the sun was sinking fast, giving long shadows to the arguing players. Looking over the darkening tree branches, I could just about see the distant tip of the Washington Monument poking at the clouds. I had many questions. I knew Ike, and that one answer always led to one more question, so I decided to stay silent and let him do all the hard work.

"You came back."

"I was plumb lucky."

Now Grandpa was squinting far into the distance at the barely visible point of the monument too. His answers were so quiet and short, he seemed to have lost all his skill in solving prickly problems. I began to worry. I wanted to tell Grandpa that this was another Ike trap that he had to escape, but my throat began to close up. Now I didn't want Ike to ask any more questions, none, zero, zip . . . and then I wanted him to ask one more.

"Is Daddy lucky?"

Grandpa's arms spread and lifted. His exaggerated shadow on the walkway made him look like a huge eagle about to fly away. But instead of leaving us, his arms flapped down onto our shoulders and pulled us in tight to his sides.

Say "yes," Grandpa. Say "absolutely one hundred percent lucky."

"Certainly he is, he has you two great kids."

His body felt warm and reassuring, but his arm on

my shoulder didn't feel like a wing anymore. Instead, it felt like a weight. His coat had hitched up his wrist, exposing the faded smear of red-and-black ink under his skin. I looked up to him in hopes of a smile, a wink, and a squeeze of encouragement, but his jaw was set and his eyes narrowed as if he was getting ready for a fight.

"Come."

The deep creases in his forehead smoothed and his face slight-softened. His knees cracked as he straightened his legs to stand.

"It's getting dark. We better get going before your mom starts to worry."

He eased us off the bench and turned us onto the right path toward home.

Vulture

It's hard to decide which bird is uglier, Vera my vulture or my newest but X-tinct stuffed dodo, which I decided to name X-it because there are no names I can think of that start with X. X-it is a word that I think sort of sounds like a first name anyway.

* ❋ *

It was late when Grandpa bumped up our driveway. Ike and I slumped in the backseat, exhausted from our adventurous day. Slowly, we got out of the car. Mom was thrilled to hear about our new carousel record. She awarded hugs and kisses, and called, "Wash up and get into your pj's," as we slouched into the house.

"We had extra-large sodas . . ."

". . . and big salt pretzels," I added, trying to signal Ike to end the list of food right there by having my voice go up on the "zels" in "pretzels," but Ike Sense prevailed.

"And then three candy bars . . ."

"Ike . . ." I tried to stop him as Mom's smile slow-vanished with each of Ike's boasts.

*   *   *

Hearing the day's completely sugarcoated menu, Mom shot us a Swishback frown that made me want to dry up like a fallen leaf.

"Well, Grandpa said it was okay," shouted Ike, and stormed off to avoid her glare.

This was the first example of excellent Ike Sense I had ever witnessed, since I was now alone to hear and bear, "Esmerelda, you should know better."

That night, because of all the day's excitement, I couldn't get comfortable in my bed. I plumped and pushed my pillow until it was bruised black-and-blue.

And that night, because of all the day's sugar, I couldn't fall asleep.

I tossed and turned, tight-twisting the sheets.

That night, because of a bad dream, I couldn't stay asleep.

I opened my eyes and sat up like a wound-up, popped out jack-in-the-box.

I couldn't really say exactly which it was that awoke me: the day's excitement, the candy's sugar, or the night's bad dream. It was probably an awful mixing of all three.

Half awake, I reached for my blankie and got a handful of rough washcloth instead.

*   *   *

Just then, a long-fingered black hand scratched at my window. Now, wide-woken by this scary sound, I caught my breath. It was only a branch that tap-tapped at the pane. I squeezed Vera hard.

Footsteps? My head swiveled to the door. Silence. There are no such things as ghosts. I know that. Ike probably couldn't sleep either. In four seconds I would hear the rush of his pee shooting into the toilet bowl. *Please, Ike, lift up the seat,* I thought.

I stared at the knuckle-sized night-light plugged in next to my dollhouse at the base of the wall. It made the miniature doll kitchen glow a warm fuzzy orange as if the sun were setting outside its window. Inside, all my dolls were fast asleep. One — two — three — four. Nothing. Total night quiet. It must be Ike. Maybe he was sick. Better check. I side-slid from under my covers. I heard the muffled sound of some of the animals in my bedzoo tumbling to the floor. *It must be Ike.* My bare feet shuffled across bristled rug. *It must be Ike.* I opened wide the door. Darkness, nothing more, no Ike, no Mom, no . . . maybe Dad came home early! The thought tingled down from the tip of my head to numb my toes. What day was it . . . ? What night . . . ? I glanced over my shoulder at my moon-streaked calendar. No. There were too many empty days left to circle. It couldn't be Dad.

*   *   *

I padded past the family photos that hung on the wall: me cuddled in a carriage in Korea, Ike swaddled in a bright-colored blanket in Kenya, Ike and me enjoying Germany, uniformed Dad hugging bundled Mom in Alaska. . . . Tick-tock, tick-tock, could that cuckoo clock be any louder? I froze. Grandpa McCarther and my newly uniformed dad shaking hands. Big smiles. Mom and Dad dressed to marry. Bigger kisses. Grandma Swishback and me with the big pink-and-blue-striped blanket. I wished I had it now. I unfroze and quick-turned into my parents' room. Deep into dark I stared. Maybe he came home early? Maybe the war was over? Maybe the war wasn't over and they sent him home early because he was . . . hurt? Soldiers get hurt. A million maybes. The rustling of the purple curtains broke my fearful silence.

"Dad," I hardly whispered. No reply.

I noisily moved to the bedside. When I was little, I would crawl between the two long sleeping mounds. When I was sick or scared of thunder they would let me sleep in that warm green-blanketed valley between them.

In the dim light I struggled to see. Needlepoint pillows propped against the headboard, cool sheets flat — no mounds of snoring grown-ups rising off the bed. No valley. I was alone in my parents' room.

And then I was really scared.

*   *   *

As I ran out and down the hall, a scream leaked down the back of my throat. Just before it spurted out, the fluttering lamp glow at the bottom of the stairs plugged it. I was safe. The kitchen light was on. Gripping the smooth banister with both hands, I single-stepped down. A still shadow stretched long across the floor.

Asleep, hair pulled in a long pony just like mine, head slumped over table, cradled on crossed slender arms just like mine, surrounded by crumpled wads and piled paper, was my mom. Napoleon raised his floppy head from the floor and stared back at me as if awaiting an order. I didn't know whether she would want me to wake her or not. I hate that feeling when you're not sure what a parent would *want* you to do. What was the right thing? Should I wake her so she could go to her bed or let her sleep because she was so tired? Sometimes you can seesaw back and forth on a problem like this until your head, heart, and stomach start to hurt.

"Mom," I breathed. I didn't mean to, it just skated out.

She looked so alone. So tired. I started to inch back to my room. Her eyes slow-lifted.

"Hey, pumpkin . . . you okay?"

"I couldn't fall asleep. I had a bad dream."

She cat-stretched, stood, put her arm around my shoulder, and gently turned me around.

"Come on, baby, I'll tuck you in."

Walrus

Whenever my dad comes into my room to kiss me good-night and I happen to be holding Wallace my walrus, he sings, "I am the walrus, coo-coo-ka-choo." He is not a walrus. I don't know why he sings this. He says it is a line from a famous song. I think that it must be a very funny song because walruses can't really sing and because of the "coo-coo-ka-choo" part.

* ❋ *

The sheets had gotten cold without me and I shivered a little as Mom pushed the edges tight under, then returned the fallen members of my bedzoo — Mandrake, Tililah, Reginald, and Gabriella — at my feet.

"Esme? You okay?"

As I nodded, my chin pushed the blanket down, and the back of my head dug deeper into the feathery pillow.

"You okay?" I parroted, squeezing my vulture.

She nodded.

"Why were you sleeping in the kitchen?"

"Just too tired."

She smiled but not a happy type, ran her hand down her ponied hair, and then sat on the side of my bed. Unlike Dad, she barely pressed down into the mattress. The just-replaced animals at the foot of my bed didn't move — not even a shudder or shake. They just stared.

"More importantly, missy, why weren't you sleeping?"

"Not too tired."

"It's hard sometimes, hmm. You know, you have done quite a bit for our country. You realize what that makes you, don't you?"

I didn't.

"A hero."

"No. Daddy is a . . ."

"Esme, you are my hero. You have been so brave and sacrificed so much during these last few months."

I felt tears creeping from the tops of my cheeks.

"Sometimes moms are sooo busy that they don't have time to tell you that they have noticed, but I have. I have. When Daddy comes back we'll have a grand ceremony and give you a medal."

"I don't want a medal. I just want . . ." And I stopped, barely letting "want" dribble out. I figured that saying what I wanted wasn't necessary and wouldn't be at all brave.

"Before you know it he'll be the one tucking you in."

She smoothed the covers where she had just sat, as if not to leave a trace, and planted a good-night forehead kiss.

"How do you know for sure?" I soft-asked.

She tapped her forefinger forcefully against the side of her head as she drifted toward the door and replied, "Kidneys, my girl, kidneys."

I wasn't so sure what she meant by it, because that is where we keep our brains, not our kidneys. She smiled to let me in on the joke. I smiled to tell her I thought it was funny. So we both were smiling.

As my mother, Penelope Lulu Swishback McCarther, backed away into the black darkness of my room and I faded down into the grays of sleep, I realized that my dad, August Aloysius McCarther the Third, was only the second strongest, bravest person alive.

X-tinct bird, Dodo

X-tinct, x-it, x-actly! *Ms. Pitcher taught us that all these X words in real life are spelled E-x, not just the letter X. She used the word* extra *as an exciting example. I still call my Dodo X-it. Sometimes I can be awful stubborn.*

* ✦ *

A rocket ship countdown can be really exciting: 10, 9, 8, 7, 6, 5, 4, 3, 2, 1 — BLAST OFF!!! The engines burp fire and launch the astronauts into the blue sky, heading to the moon. My countdown isn't as exciting. 1 week, 7 days, 168 hours, a mess of minutes, lots and lots of seconds (more "than you can shake a stick at") — DAD'S HOME!!!

It's less like my head going into the clouds and more like having the ocean in my stomach. Some days the waves are so rough it makes me seasick. I feel like running into my bathroom, lying over the toilet, and throwing up. But I can't. I hate that feeling when you want to puke but you can't. Ugh.

*   *   *

Martina's mom was stuck in Mobile tending her sick grandmother for the weekend. This was bad for her mom and even worse for her grandma but great for Martina and me since she got to sleep over.

Mom was making pasta for dinner and we were super hungry. Standing on chairs staring down at the pot of water on the stove, Martina and I watched, waiting for it to boil so we could drop in our handfuls of spaghetti.

"A watched pot never boils," Mom warned, then wandered away.

"You think it knows we are watching?" asked Martina.

"How could water know if it is being watched? That's silly."

We peered in for a second more, then at the same time both of us inched backward on our chairs and ducked down below the pot's edge, out of sight of the water.

"Whatcha doing?" asked Ike when he entered.

"Shhhhh," we showered down on him. His ears turned Ike-red and he moved double time to find Mom. After a few moments we inched up, and sure enough, big bubbles were shooting off the bottom.

"It's boiling!" I squealed.

"Mrs. McCarther! It's boiling!" Martina reeled.

"Penny," my mom corrected, and helped direct the paths of our hard pasta into the pot's erupting center.

"Hmm, I guess a watched pot does boil."

Martina and I nodded and smiled but did not offer anything to make her think different. Sometimes it is better for parents not to know they are almost always right.

After dinner we all got into our pj's, cuddled up on the couch in the den under a huge Grandma Swishback quilt, made loads of popcorn, and watched an ancient not-color movie about a woman who really, really likes a ghost and also really, really likes a real live man. Partway in Ike got bored and grumped up the stairs, mumbling, "Dumb movie." I was happy about him leaving because it made the movie better and left us more popcorn.

For sleepovers, Dad would carry the mattress from the downstairs guest bedroom and set it on the floor next to my bed. I always thought this task must have been awfully easy because with little fuss the mattress always appeared, sheets hospital-cornered, pillows plumped, ready for my friend to be tucked in. I was wrong. It was way easier for Dad to do than to actually be done.

The three of us dragged the flopping mattress down the hall and lifted it onto the first step. With our backs bent, Martina and I gripped the top and Mom the bottom.

"Pull," Mom commanded, and we did.

"Push!" we called down, and she did.

It took about a hundred *pulls* and *pushes,* combined with several laughs, a bunch of giggles, and many more grunts to gradually, step by step, inch by inch, make it to the top of the stairs. Sweaty-wet, Mom flopped onto the mattress. We followed.

"Your dad is going to pay when he gets home! This is entirely one hundred percent his job."

"Yeah, he's going to totally pay," I agreed.

"Absolutely pay," chimed Martina, not wanting to be left out.

Pushing and pulling the mattress to its proper spot next to my bed, we listed every job we would have Dad do when he returned.

Mom tucked the pink sheets under the corners and went to get the extra pillow.

I handed Martina Karl the monkey from my bedzoo.

"Want to borrow him for the night?"

"Oh, Karl! How have you been getting along?" She put his puckered mouth to her ear. "Really! Wonderful."

It was true, he had gotten along with all, from Alvin to Zelda — even though his first name did not start with an M.

*   *   *

Safely sandwiched between the sheets, I positioned my kind-of-ugly dodo, whose turn it was for me to cuddle. I explained exactly why the dodo bird really started with the letter X and Martina gasp-laughed at Grandpa's problem-letter solution.

"You know odd is almost dodo spelled backward," I reminded her.

"Almost," agreed Martina.

"Okay, you two. Time to quiet down and get some sleep."

Mom swept in, tucked the covers to our chins, and gave us kisses.

"Are you all right, Martina?"

"Yes. Thank you, Mrs. McCarther."

"Penny," my mom corrected, and flipped the lights. "Sleep, ladies. No more talking."

Both of us squeezed our eyes shut. The door creaked closed. Slippered footsteps traveled the stairs. Our eyes popped open. *No more talking, indeed,* I thought to myself. Then why bother having a sleepover! I turned on my left side, and Martina turned on her right side to face me. Lit only by the tiny flicker of the night-light, our super-serious sleepover whisperings began. Voices barely louder than breathing, we chatted about our spaghetti dinner, the ghostly movie, and my pesky Ike. Then, after several exhausted yawns, we went silent and tried to fall asleep.

I couldn't. Wondering if Martina could, I leaned over. Ulrich my unicorn, Gabriella my goat, and a small herd of other fluffy animals that I could not exactly identify hopped from my bedzoo to the floor. I stared down into the dark shadows. The watery whites of Martina's open eyes glistened. She was most definitely awake.

"Martina?" I whispered. There was no response. "Martina?" I slightly raised the volume.

"Will they come home?"

"Soon for you. Eighteen days." We all knew each other's parents' return dates better than our multiplication tables.

"Seventeen, it's after midnight."

I glanced at the glowing red numbers that sat on my desk. It was way past my bedtime.

"Richie C. said that when you see a single shoe, sneaker, or boot hanging from a tree or sitting in the street it's because a lot of soldiers come home only needing one and they throw the other out. Do you think that is . . ."

Her voice slid short to silence. I clear-remembered our wonderful day parading around the neighborhood collecting scrap metal and laughing at the sidesplitting stories we had made up about all those single shoes.

"Fustilug."

"You called old Mr. Wormser that. What is that? What's a . . . ?"

"Fustilug — it rhymes with crusty bug."

Martina quarter-chuckled at my one-line poem. Then I told her about the deep dark jungle of Nostomania and the bandy-legged blue bugs that live there.

"They crawl into asleep people's ears, people who don't think very much even when they are awake, and spin brain webs that gum up the whole thinking works."

Martina's mouth slow-slacked open and her eyes became full mooned.

"Then forever after, they have to say out loud whatever comes into their head, no matter how hurtful it is to others."

"Wow. I didn't know. . . ."

"Fustilugs live miserably, wandering from town to town without friends, 'cause whatever they think, they say. It is all so very sad and we really must feel sorry for them."

"Fustilugs." Martina yawned and closed her eyes.

I felt tiredness tug at me as well, and whole-closed my eyes. Before falling deep into my nightly dream I barely heard Martina whisper, "You're a good storyteller."

Yak

I got Yolanda from a complete stranger. After we moved to Alexandria we bought a car out on the highway at Yakima's Used Cars. Johnny Yakima, the owner, gives little stuffed yaks with the name of his company printed on the belly so you always remember where your car came from. I think this is a good idea because now I will never forget where I got Yolanda my yak.

* ☼ *

We excitedly colored in signs and hung decorations.

"Why does he stay one more day than night?" I asked while I scrawled a big pink W.

"Because there is always one more day than night," answered Ike, displaying classic Ike Sense.

"Hmmmm, well, maybe," my mom hummed, "but probably the army just wants him to be rested so he's ready to play with you right when he returns."

Hmmmm, I hummed to myself. After exactly one hundred days and ninety-nine nights, I wanted to see him, ready — or not.

*   *   *

We sat waiting on our stoop, our bent legs propping up our scrawled sign, WELCOME HOME, DADDY! People honked their horns as they passed. Mom said it was their way of saying congratulations.

Mrs. Wood creakily crossed to us holding a telltale tin.

"Can't stay to talk, but I brought some gingersnaps to hold you over. Be sure to save at least one for the returning doughboy."

We agreed that we absolutely would.

"Ever find out why?" she asked as she made her way away.

We were completely baffled by her question and there was no disguising our confused expressions.

"Doughboys! Young Isaac. Why were they called doughboys?" she crackled as she retreated down our path.

Ike had not attempted to look up this particular *why.*

"Don't think I've forgotten, young man. Next time our paths cross I expect a proper answer."

Determinedly pushing her shopping cart down the block, she vanished as fast as she had arrived.

It started to drizzle and the pink W in WELCOME started to run away. There were far fewer honks. And my imagination started to run away as well. I started to worry. I started to worry about every big thing and every little thing. I started to worry that the rain would keep his plane from landing. I started to worry that I had miscounted the days. I started to worry that old Mr. Wormser would walk past, his cane kicking out in front onto his dark shadowed path, and he would stop and say something nasty and I would start to cry. I worried . . .

Then, as the clouded sun wandered low down the sky, he came marching: my hero, my dad, duffel over shoulder, smile on lips, raindrops streaming down cheeks.

I dropped the sign and ran. He ran. We hugged hard as if to make up for each and every hug we had missed while he was away.

Ike, charging like a little bull, yelled over and over, "Daddy! Daddy! Daddy!"

He engulfed us both in his broad arms. Napoleon circled, barking, rattling his chain, shaking his wet coat, swatting our faces with his swinging tail.

I carefully checked off each part of him from his fuzzy buzz cut down to his two tight-laced combat boots, and all were exactly the same as when he left.

"I didn't forget," he whispered, pressing the frayed bunch of blankie into my hand.

Embarrassed because now raindrops streamed down my cheeks, I buried my eyes in his rough, red burned neck and replied, "Neither did I."

Zebra

The night I cuddle with my Zelda it means one thing: I've reached the end the alphabet. Which means one thing — my dad is home!

* ⊙ *

We wrestled over our hugs and kisses to get inside. As we curled into the kitchen, Ike and I alternated telling about all the amazing adventures that we had over the past one hundred days and ninety-nine nights. We told him about the big events, like the school play and our day with Grandpa McCarther, and the little ones, like what we ate for dinner and how much homework we had. Napoleon barked at the end of each story as if to add an exclamation point. We left out all of the bad things. No need to worry him on his very first day home. No need to make him sad on his very first day home. No need to scare him away on his very first day home!

*   *   *

When Ike and I became breathless, Mom would chime in with some detail that we had forgotten or tell something that she did or had to do or that he had to do. Then all of a sudden, as if all the words we had in our brains were sucked out and sealed away, we went silent. Dad sat staring at us and we at him. For now, we really didn't have anything more to tell him. It was his turn to tell us about his adventures. But he just sat.

"What was your war like, Daddy?" It wasn't what I meant to say but that was the way it came out.

"Esme!" Mommy blurted, making me feel like a fustilug of the first order.

Dad let out a little laugh, the kind that told me that although I didn't ask the question exactly right, he knew what I meant and it was okay by him. Ike excitedly dove off his chair and landed on the couch next to Dad.

"Did you shoot anyone and did they shoot you?" He asked, in a humongously bad display of Ike Sense.

"Ike!" Mom exclaimed, trying to control a moment that was now out of control.

"Well . . . ," he started slowly, "in the day it was hotter than Kenya and at night it was colder than Korea. It was very, very boring. We sat around a lot, waiting. And when we were not waiting we were walking through the biggest sandbox you could imagine."

"Neat," poked Ike.

"But you could never make castles out of the sand, not a single one, because there was no water so it wouldn't ever stick. All I did the whole entire time, every second of every minute of every day, was try to figure out ways to get back home."

"And you did it!" I shouted.

"And now you'll never have to go back again," stated Ike.

There was a whole bowl of silence.

"I won't lie to you, Ike. I might have to go back."

"Why?"

That was a favorite Ike question. He could ask that question over and over until an adult would just finally yell, "Because!" and walk away. I have to say that this time I was glad Ike asked "Why?" because I was think-ing the same exact question over and over in my head. *Whywhywhywhy?*

"I don't think this is the time . . . ," Mom started.

"Because there are a lot of my friends still there and the army may send me to help them."

"And it is your duty to go."

"Exactly, Esme."

I expected Ike to ask "Why?" yet again, in typical Ike fashion, but he didn't.

"I understand," he said instead.

"You two have certainly grown up while I was gone," he proud-said, but looked nearly sad.

*   *   *

Dad hardly lifted his duffel and dragged it toward the stairs. It seemed heavier than before, as if he had brought home pounds and pounds of sand from the desert. Napoleon, tail flipping like a windshield wiper, neck chain happily jingle-bell jangling, trailed after him. Mom gave us hugs that told us she would be right back.

Ike and I sat looking at each other. He started an awful out-of-tune whistle and I gave him my harshest Swish-back frown, which immediately took the whistle right out of him. The room was nearly dark but I was too tired to flip on lights. The ticktock of the cuckoo clock, the heavy thud of the dropped duffel, muffled voices, then the clomping sound of his boots flooded down the stairs, trailed by a trickle of Mom's softer click-clacking shoes. He appeared in front of us, framed in the door.

"You guys must be starving."

We were.

"I thought we would go out to eat to celebrate." Mom appeared from behind and slow-floated her hand into Dad's.

"Are you kidding?" he boomed. "It took me one hundred days and ninety-nine nights to get back into this house, and right now I'm not taking one single step out!"

I felt a warm feeling gurgle inside my growling stomach and start to heat up the rest of my body until my face felt flushed red. Ike pinballed back and forth on the couch, which he was usually not allowed to do, and was ready to rocket out the roof if Dad didn't soon grab him.

"Well, come on, let's get to work," he ordered, then scooped me up in his robin redbreasted arm and lowered his back to Ike, who grabbed his neck for the short ride into the kitchen. I have already mentioned that the kitchen is the single most important room in our house because it is where we do our important cooking and all our serious talking.

"I didn't have time to shop, there's not a thing for dinner!" Mom warned. Then, knowing that there were only lonely crumbs of food scattered about the fridge and that we would be eating ketchup over cookies and mayo mixed with mustard, she added, "How about we order in?"

But before you could say flour or flower, pots were clanging, spoons were tinkling, eggs were crackin', and we all — me, Ike, Mom, and Dad — were laughing and cooking away as if the many days and hardly fewer nights had been no longer than a five-minute trip to the corner store.

"Spaaatulllaaa, spa-chew — la, sssspit-u-laaa." He rolled the word until we were happily rolling across the floor.

*   *   *

That night my father, August Aloysius McCarther the Third, a sergeant in the United States Army, cooked pancakes for dinner, which was an absolute McCarther family first. I can tell you that without doubt they were the top-dog tastiest pancakes ever made.

August Aloysius McCarther the Third's Top Secret Rules for Top-Dog Tasty Pancakes

1 egg
1 cup yogurt
1/4 cup water
1 tablespoon oil
1 cup flour
1 teaspoon salt
1 teaspoon baking soda

1. Mix up all the wet stuff. Try not to make a mess.

2. Now mix up all the dry things. Remember — flour, not flower!

3. Add the dry stuff to the wet stuff and careful-mix them together.

4. Now from here on out you absolutely need a grown-up's help
   They heat a frying pan and drop in some butter. Sizzle!

5. After the butter melts, spoon circles of batter out. The more
   batter, the bigger the pancake. Don't make them too big or they
   are hard to flip.

6. When little bubbles start popping, flip the pancakes with a
   spaaatula, spitula, spatuuuulaaa.

7. When light brown on each side, they are ready.

8. Eat with gobs of syrup.